SO NEAR, SO FAR...

Written by Thanos Papatzitzes

SO NEAR, SO FAR…

translated by
Dr. Dimitris Thanasoulas

Pharos Books

ISBN: 978-93-55462-33-6
eISBN: 978-93-55462-41-1

© Publishers

Publisher: Pharos Books (P) Ltd.
Plot No.-55, Main Mother Dairy Road
Pandav Nagar, East Delhi-110092 (India)
Phone: +014049995474
WhatsApp: +014049995474
E-mail: sales@pharosbooks.in
Website: www.pharosbooks.in
Edition: 2022

SO NEAR, SO DAR...
Author: Thanos Papatzitzes

This book is dedicated to my only daughter Nectaria.

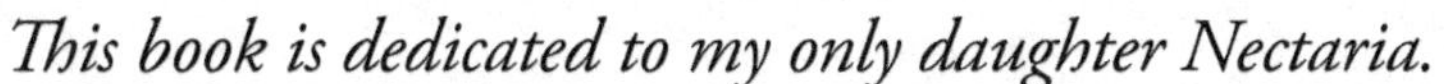

Having made a contribution to Medicine for 40 years, gaining experience from my workplace, I made a hard decision—to commit some thoughts to paper.

This is my first attempt in this extremely difficult field of book writing. Its theme has been inspired by the horror caused by the last World War, through the romance and love of two young people.

You see, these two words fit everywhere…

FOREWORD

Maybe maturity and experiences,
maybe the sounds and a glance,
maybe a moment like a flash,
and the soul that opens up
and reveals its private parts,
maybe curiosity
and expression
infiltrated by thought,
maybe emotion and a little bit of reason…
and all this together,
like the inspiration that is etched
first in mind,
then on a piece of paper…
and the result is judged
by the others,
either positively or negatively…
but you make sure you like this,
for their judgement
is the best gift
for you…

*If your life
was ripped to a thousand pieces,
cherish its moments…*

CHAPTER ONE

The summer of 1970 is scorching hot. The bus draws up in the big sandlot. It's getting dark…Anna gets off, tightly holding the hand of her daughter Helga and, just like the rest, starts going up the narrow stone alley that leads to the sacred theatre of Epidaurus.

She has been in Greece, a beautiful Mediterranean country, for the past few hours. It's a country she too has adored.

As she enters this ancient holy theatre, a young woman comes closer and gives her a leaflet that describes the play's plot that will soon begin. Anna is familiar with this play as she has graduated from the Department of Classics at the University of Berlin. It is the work of an ancient Greek tragedian that presents the life of the young son of a king, Orestes, who became a matricide when he found out that his mother and her lover murdered his father together. Through his deed, he felt he avenged himself on his father's unjust assassination. He was tried and acquitted by the Supreme Court, but he never managed to escape his remorse over his crime, regardless of his motive.

An exceptional professor, Adolf Krause, taught her this and many more works.

With her precious daughter always by her side, she sits on the big stone seat in the second row, a seat that has been standing there for thousands of years. The full moon overhead is the only light that falls on the stage. Absolute silence reigns. It is of utmost importance as this theatre's acoustics are unique worldwide, showcasing the ancient world's architectural genius.

During the ascent, Anna spoke to Helga, despite being so young, promised to be quiet. The performance has just begun…

A performance that whisks her back years ago…

Autumn of 1961. West Berlin…

"Good morning, sweetheart. It's time to wake up," Anna's mother whispered in her ear, giving her a tender kiss, as she always had ever since she held her in her arms for the first time.

Anna wearily opened her eyes, reached out to give her beloved mother a tender hug, smiled, and stayed there in her arms for a few minutes.

"You've grown up, love. You start a new life today. Today, University is opening its doors to welcome the prettiest student in the city."

"That's over the top, mum. You know how many people like me—even better than me!—will be there today?"

"For me, just like for every mother, you are the best. I want you to become someone special. Your father would be so proud of you if he were with us…" answered Mrs. Bird.

Anna wiped a teardrop that trickled down her mother's cheek, got out of bed, and made for the bathroom.

"I'll be waiting for you downstairs, sweetheart. You'll have your breakfast."

The first day, the beginning of new life, plenty of dreams…

"What will it be like?" she wondered.

The wind stroking her face is not very cold. The autumn of 1961 is milder than any other year. As she reaches the bus stop, she stops short. She doesn't get on and prefers to walk a distance. She will catch the bus at the next one.

"What will it be like today?" she wondered. "Was it a wise choice to study the Classics? But wasn't that always what lured me? I'm going to sit in the front of the amphitheatre so that I can see and hear my professors clearly," she whispered as she boarded the bus in this new chapter of her life.

In a short while, she crosses her school threshold, a grandiose building housing one of the city's most prestigious universities. Although she's a first-year student, she doesn't feel awkward and, oozing self-confidence, she walks in the direction of a stand in the second row. She sits down, with her peers' voices buzzing around her. Anna was always smiling.

"Hey, I'm Emma," she hears beside her the voice of a sweet girl, who's reaching out to shake her hand.

"Nice to meet you. I'm Anna. How d'you feel?"

"Somewhat awkward. It's the first day, you know…Do you like the field of study you chose?"

"I've always been enchanted by History and Civilisation. I was good at Classics, so I wanted to delve into Philosophy—mainly its roots. A teacher of mine often mentioned ancient Greek writers and poets, who made references to man and society."

"Yes, all this thrills me too," replies Emma, showing how much she likes Anna.

A charming man interrupted their conversation. He was in his forties and, amid that commotion, he was trying to attract their attention by raising his hands.

There was soon silence in the amphitheatre.

"Good morning. I'm Adolf Krause, one of the professors you'll have throughout your studies. I welcome you and congratulate you on your success. My colleagues and I will try to impart as much knowledge as we possibly can. The module I will be teaching is the most fundamental of all. I am referring to the Classics from antiquity to date, which will fill your mind and soul with significant knowledge. This knowledge will become a powerful weapon for the rest of your lives. Just like you now, fifteen years ago, I too decided to follow this route through the embers of that devastating war. And, believe me, as you walk along with this tough, but wonderful road to a knowledge of Classical Philosophy, you will be able to view life from a completely different perspective in the future. I don't want to weary you today as it's your first day here. We have so much time ahead of us! I'll be at your disposal. Let me welcome you once again. You're free to go today. See you tomorrow morning. Have a nice day!"

The freshmen's voices petered out in a while, and the amphitheatre was left empty.

"Anna, everyone's gone. Let's get out of here."

Engrossed in what she heard, still in her seat, as if dazed, Anna shot to her feet at Emma's touch.

"What happened?" she asked.

"You were lost in his words, eh? You had fixed your gaze upon him!" Emma replied smilingly.

"I don't know. Maybe the way he spoke..." Anna explained.

"Maybe his charm as well. Don't tell me he's not handsome..." Emma said on the spot, which made Anna blush.

After saying goodbye to the first friend she made at uni, Anna left for home. She didn't want to go back yet; she needed to walk. After all, she often did that as it really pleased her.

This first day in the new chapter of her life was wonderful. This single hour filled her with joy.

"He was marvellous! His posture, his speech, his politeness. Suppose all professors are like him...Philosophy, classical writers, and poets. I think I've made a wise choice. I'll tell mum how happy I am!" she said to herself as she got on the bus.

As if out of intuition, her mother was waiting for her at the door. Anna threw herself into her arms. Her face was radiant with joy. Mrs. Bird saw that straight away. After all, her mother was the one who brought her up; only she could feel her heart.

"As I can understand, my love, your first day at the uni was wonderful. A great philosopher once said that the beginning is half of the whole—something along these lines. I hope this day, which is your first day in your new life, will be the beginning of a happy and fulfilled life because you deserve it and deserve every good in the world. That's true, my child."

"Why are you crying, mum? Why?"

Mrs. Bird quickly wiped her tears, slightly moved back, and told her in a trembling voice:

"I'm really touched, my love, that's why. I brought you up alone with so much difficulty, and I feel proud! If your father were alive, he'd feel twice as proud as I am. You see, he died so young that you didn't have the chance to know him. Come on now. You'd better have something to eat. I've made something special for the day. You'll tell me all about your experience at the table."

"Well, mum, the School I chose is out of this world! The modules are exciting…and the first professor that turned up in the amphitheatre—the one who's going to teach us most of the modules—is a hunk! Er, I'm sorry, I meant he's an orator…" Anna said spontaneously with a slight blush, which her mother noticed.

"Ah! I forgot to say that today, the first day of my new life, I made my first friend, Emma. We took our seats, and she gave me the impression that we're a very good match!"

"Time will tell, sweetheart. I'm glad you're happy from the very first day. Be careful, though, as you're still young and impressionable."

"What I was saying, mum, is that Mr. Adolf, the professor I told you about, said he's the one to teach us the most modules throughout our studies."

"You said that before, honey. We're talking about the hunk, right? Is this his name?" Mrs. Bird asked with a sly smile.

"What does this smile of yours imply, mum? How can you think of such things?" Anna said and stood up.

"You barely touched your food, my child!" complained Mrs. Bird.

"I'm bloated, mum. I'll go upstairs to my room. I'll lie down for a while."

The following days were quiet and uneventful for Anna. In the morning, she was always in good time for her lectures. She went there earlier than anyone else to take the same seat in the same row—the second front. Emma felt closer to her. She had probably found a great friend.

Mr. Adolf Krause, the charming professor, became more and more agreeable to his students. He brought out the best in them. At least that's what Anna felt the moment she laid her eyes on him…

CHAPTER TWO

This winter is so heavy in Germany. Although not all modules are mandatory, Anna hasn't skipped a single class. She's there in the same second-row seat every day.

This morning, the whole city is covered in snow; only the highways are open. She didn't wake up on time, and Mrs. Bird let her sleep in. After a while, Anna ran down the stairs, yelling and asking her mother why she had let her oversleep.

"It's not the end of the world, darling. Today's a very cold day, so you can study at home and keep me company. After all, I suppose very few students will attend classes at the uni."

"Oh, mum, you shouldn't have done that!" Anna said smilingly. "I don't want to miss a single class. Please, make sure you wake me up on time." She glimpsed at the clock on the wall. "Luckily, the first class starts at 10 today," she whispered.

"What did you say, honey? Whose class starts at 10? Do you want to tell me something I don't know?"

"What are you talking about? No…er…All I'm saying is that Emma will be on time, and I'll be absent. That's all I'm saying…"

"Ah! Is that it?" her mother responded with a smile again.

After almost an hour, Anna arrives at her School and storms into the amphitheatre through the back door as her first class has already begun. Adolf is on the podium. So as not to make any noise, she sits in the last row. There are very few students today, and they're all sitting in the front seats. Emma is not there.

"Please sit in the front, miss. We haven't started yet. I understand it's difficult to commute today. Come. After all, your own seat is empty," Adolf's voice is heard from the far end of the hall, much to everyone's surprise. Feeling self-conscious, Anna went to her seat.

"How can he remember my seat?" she wondered. "Does he remember everyone else's seats? That's impossible!"

"Well, my dear children, today I'm going to tell you about a notion and an act called revenge, an act that can simply cause a bad situation or even lead to murder. I'm going to go deeper into that through an ancient drama written by one of the most significant tragedians in ancient Greece. This play is a tragedy called 'Medea,' which seeks to show us how affront and rejection can make a man commit a crime. The main person of this tragedy is Medea, daughter of a king, who fell in love with and got married to a prince, with whom she had two children. Yet, at some point, her fate leads her to the role of the wife who has been rejected by her husband when she finds out that Jason, in order to win the throne of a flourishing city—marries the daughter of its king and asks Medea to leave. Then, her soul is gripped by passion as all her life expectations have been dashed. Out of love and with stars in her eyes, she followed him from the Asian hinterland, leaving behind her father's kingdom. This profound sorrow leads her soul from one stage to the next, and in the end, she takes revenge by killing the king and his daughter and, after failing to kill her husband, she ends up murdering her own children."

While listening to him, Anna was pinned to her seat, engrossed in the topic and his words.

"This story sounds simple and common," Adolf continued. "Yet, here, the writer focuses more on whether you can justify her decision in a similar act of violence. He wants to point out that the feelings that grip the human psyche can sometimes clash so violently that they can even lead to utter destruction. As it's already late, though, I will close by saying that Medea committed this heinous crime in order to deprive her husband of his offspring, even if she would lose it too. I will say no more since this tragedy will be thoroughly analysed next year."

The murmur that was heard as a reaction interrupted Adolf, who said: "This as well as other equally admirable works that will be analysed are long and timeless. You've had a foretaste today. Please study this work and I would like to hear your own take on it over the following days. Have a nice day!"

For Anna, this had been the best day so far. She remained seated for a few minutes and plunged into thought again. The play's themes, which Adolf presented so vividly, rubbed off on her for no apparent reason. But was it only this?

"He addressed me today," she thought. "And he remembered my seat. Could it be…? Well, I attended class despite the bad weather. I didn't want to miss his lecture. Why? What's the matter with me? No, it's nothing…," she said to herself and leapt to her feet as if snapping out of a dream. The amphitheatre was empty now, and from the end of the corridor came the voices of those attending the next class. She picked up her bag and left hurriedly.

As she got out in the street, she felt the need to walk to the next bus station like she often did. Still, the biting cold forced her to get on the bus. She felt on top of the world. But why?

"Is it the lecture? I don't think so. After all, the topic was so heavy and depressing…And I have plenty of time to delve into it. Then, what's going on?" she wondered again. "Could it be him? My professor? No, it can't be. This is not supposed to be happening to me."

Her heart was pounding for the first time. The next stop announcement, though, brought her back to reality with a bump. She hopped off the bus somewhat perplexed and, quickening her gait—almost at a run—, she walked into her place and went straight to her room.

Over the following days, the weather got worse, and the university closed down for a while. Anna was cooped up at home, poring over her books and talking to her friend Emma on the phone. Anna didn't tell her anything about the incident in the amphitheatre; she kept it under wraps. However, Mrs. Bird didn't fail to notice how nervous she was to have stayed in all these days.

One morning, her mother broaches the subject for the first time.

"Sweetheart, I see you've been kind of restless these days. What's the matter?"

"No, mum, I'm alright. Why d'you say that?"

"Maybe you miss going to school. It's still early. Don't rush. All things come at the right time in life. How are you and Emma doing?"

"We're doing great, mum. She's a very nice girl, and I think I've made a very good friend."

"What about the…handsome professor?"

"He's fine! But why are you asking this?" Anna replied Anna brusquely, unable to hide her slight blush.

"What's that supposed to mean?" insisted Mrs. Bird.

"Well, that day I overslept, er…he addressed me and I was so happy about it! I mean… he paid attention to me. He's seen how diligent I am…"

"Well done, my child! I'm so happy for you!" answered her mother with a knowing smile. "I heard on the radio that the weather is getting better, so I guess tomorrow or the day after tomorrow, schools are going to open up again."

Anna had already walked into the library. She had to study that play Adolf had so beautifully analysed the other day. Passion, revenge, murder… "Can such a thing happen these days? Was the world different back then? Can a soul calm down after such a crime, even if it's committed for a reason? Can someone get away with such an act?"

She had to study all this today so as to be ready for the next couple of days. She also had to write down some questions to ask him…

The weather was getting better, and life got back to normal. Anna was always on time, especially after that morning, something seemed to have changed deep inside her. His image followed her like a shadow. Still, she hesitated to approach him. It was like a fear she couldn't put her finger on.

Winter gave place to spring. It was already April. This morning, Anna is determined. She thinks she has a loose end to tie up. First, she has to get some answers. Something inside of her urges her to approach him independently, and her beloved 'Medea' gives her this opportunity.

"Professor, may I?"

"Please, miss. What's your name?"

"Anna. Anna Meisner. I'd like to ask you something. May I?"

"With pleasure, Miss Anna, but don't stand there in the corridor. Please come into my office."

Reserved and with her head bowed, which was so unlike her as she was quite daring, she followed him. His office seemed quite cramped to her, but Adolf's cordial voice made her feel at home.

"Well, Miss Anna, I'm all ears, after I tell you that I have the ability to observe and remember my students' faces. However, I haven't been teaching for very long. To make you feel at home, I will tell you that you are very diligent. You are very attentive during my lectures and always take the same seat in the second row, right opposite the podium."

Adolf's words seemed to bring Anna out of her shell and make her speak.

"Thank you for your kind words, professor. I've meant to ask you a few things regarding Medea, but I've hesitated to see you. Well, it's been quite some time since that cold day in the amphitheatre. On the other hand, I don't want to weary you. You already have enough on your plate so that you won't remember it."

"Don't be so sure!" Adolf replied spontaneously. "As I said, I remember very well—especially the things I'm interested in."

Blushing and feeling joyful all of a sudden, Anna answered:

"Yes…I remember that morning very well, and I'll never forget your kindness. Shall I ask you a few things?"

"Well, Medea, my dear Anna, is a wonderful play, but so difficult to analyse. I gave you the gist of it, which grapples with revenge. I gave you the opportunity to study it for next year as it's going to be a mandatory module. We'll delve into it then. The ancient tragedians influenced subsequent playwrights like Shakespeare and many others. As far as I'm concerned, I'm in love with Classical Philosophy, and I've visited Greece in the summertime and again to attend these plays performed by Greek and foreign directions in the two world-renowned ancient theatres."

Dumbfounded by his words, mainly the way he uttered them, Anna raised her eyes and, as if unable to check herself, she fixed them into his own. Now it was Adolf's turn to feel awkward; still, he leapt to his feet and carried on:

"Therefore, Medea, my dear Anna, is the personification of revenge—any kind of revenge. It shows how far a human being's passion can go. She thought she would purge her soul through this act, thus serving her own sense of right and wrong. In another tragedy, 'The Oresteia,' we will analyse another notion that of remorse haunting a human after a crime—if he feels remorse, and if he can avoid it."

"Professor, you've covered me within a few minutes," Anna replied with enthusiasm, unable to tear her eyes from his. "Sorry to take up your time. I know how precious it is. Now I must go. Thank you so much!"

"No problem, my dear Anna. You should know I'm very happy about this meeting. My students don't take such an interest. The term is drawing to a close in a few days. I will bid you farewell in a couple of weeks and wish you all 'Happy Summer.' Well, I'll wish you now, Anna. May you have a great summer!" he told her, giving her a firm handshake.

Anna felt her hand burning so much; she was about to faint. She almost ran out of his office, her heart pounding. She stepped out to breathe in some fresh air, but that wasn't enough.

"What's the matter with me?" she wondered. "This can't be happening. I guess it's a nightmare I will soon snap out of. It was just a casual teacher-student meeting where I had the opportunity to get the answers I needed. Nothing else, but he kept saying 'my dear Anna.' What does that mean? What is it I'm feeling right now? No! I just imagine things. I'll be OK soon." But her heart was in that office, with that man, and she had no control over it. Maybe she didn't even want to have control over it.

"Is this what love is like?" she wondered as she walked into her house.

CHAPTER THREE

Only a few days are left till the end of the academic year. On the one hand, Anna is happy that holidays are just around the corner, but on the other, she is sad it will take her some time to get back to school. Something has surely changed within. At the same time, she is gripped by a kind of fear like she is keeping under wraps a precious secret so that nobody will find out. On the other hand, this meeting with the professor hasn't only made her heart pound, which is so unprecedented for her, but also given her soul quite an impetus. As if she suddenly grew up. All day long, Adolf's on her mind. So is he in her dreams? And the more she thinks of him, the bigger her fear.

"What if all this is a figment of my imagination? What if he doesn't feel anything for me? Maybe I should speak to someone who could help me. Emma, perhaps? No, I shouldn't panic right now. Mum shouldn't get wind of that, either. It's better to speak to Emma, my best friend. What if she sees all this as a joke and makes fun of me?" she thought. "No, it's still early. Maybe all this will be my own wish—nothing else. He's an eminent and rich scientist—at least, that's what people are saying at the uni—, and I'm sure he'll have a strict family. I don't even know if he feels anything for me. It's also this age difference between us and, although it's well known that he's not married, he could probably be having an affair with a woman from his environment."

That was the last day of the academic year. Much calmer now, Anna took her seat in the amphitheater quite early, which surprised Emma.

That was the last lecture, and Adolf was on time. As soon as he got on the podium, Anna fixed her gaze upon him. Seeing that he was looking at her too, she felt shivers up and down her spine. And this got only worse when Emma nudged her knowingly.

Clearing his throat, Adolf addressed his 'children,' saying good morning.

"As you well know, today's our last day. I would like to thank you on behalf of the other professors for your presence and diligence throughout the year. You did quite well in the exams, but I want to point out that the girls over there did much better," he said smilingly, his eyes falling on Anna, which gave her goosebumps again.

"I'm here to tell you a few things: you gained lots of knowledge throughout this year. It's up to you to retain as much of it as possible. See you next autumn, when a new year begins with harder modules—harder, but more fascinating. Don't get all worked up about that! I want you to get some rest, have fun, and prepare yourselves. I wish you a happy holiday season."

Just as Adolf walked out of the amphitheatre, Anna, as if on the spur of the moment, shot to her feet and ran behind him, without caring about the others' presence.

"Professor, excuse me."

Adolf didn't seem to be surprised like he was expecting it.

"Yes, my dear Anna," he told her tenderly. "Should you need anything, please come to my office in five minutes. This is not the right place."

Anna only had the time to nod her head. She didn't really have anything to tell him. She couldn't understand why she ran behind him. Those five minutes seemed like an eternity to her. She nervously paced up and down the corridor and hid the moment she saw Emma looking for her in the corner. Exactly five minutes later, not giving a damn about her classmates' curious glances, she knocked on Adolf's office door. He welcomed her with a broad smile, this time with more familiarity. His face seemed even more handsome to her. He rose from his seat, shook her hand, and asked her to sit.

"I'm all ears, Miss Anna," Adolf cut to the chase, sounding more formal, which struck Anna as odd.

"Er…you know, I didn't mean to tell you anything in particular. Well…I don't know why. I just wanted to wish you a happy summer in person," she replied, suddenly regaining her composure.

"My dear Anna," Adolf sounded more cordial now, "I want to tell you that you've excelled yourself this year. This was surely tiring as you didn't miss a single lecture—even on that snowy day, you came in late. You see, I have an exceptional memory. I want you to rest this summer, and let me repeat that the new academic year will be really tough. As I know you're about to ask me about this, I'll say that next year we are going to go deeper into the heroine's mental state, which we have left incomplete…"

As if magically mustering up courage, Anna looked him in the eyes again, saying that she would get some rest and prepare herself for the next year.

"Where are you going on holiday? I suppose with your parents."

"I don't know yet. I'll decide on that with my mother. It depends on our savings, of course. Ever since my father passed away—I was two years old—, my mother has made sure I want for nothing."

"I'm sorry to hear that, but you should know that there are worse things in life. Unfortunately, at the end of the war, I lost both my parents, and for several years I lived with my aunt—my father's sister. She lives on her own now. Let's not talk about such unpleasant things right now. Maybe we'll have the chance to do that some other time."

"Yes, that's right. May I…ask if you live on your own? Sorry to be so indiscreet…"

"Yes, completely alone," Adolf answered on the spot with a knowing smile.

"Where are you going on holiday? If that's not too indiscreet on my part, that is…" asked Anna again, regaining her composure.

"Ah, my dear, this year, I'll be visiting Athens. A Greek academic has invited me. He teaches Philosophy. As he said, he has a surprise for me—a ticket to an ancient performance at one of the most renowned theatres under the Parthenon. I'd like to tell you about all this, but we have plenty of time on our hands," replied Adolf, instantly forgetting that he was a professor.

"I'm sorry. It's my fault. I came here for no reason, but I'd love to hear you speaking for hours," she responded without any hesitation. She stood up, reached out her hand to shake his, and Adolf like a real gentleman, rose from his seat, held her hand, and looked her in the eyes again with the self-assurance of a mature man, saying:

"I'm so glad to see you here today. When I come back from my holiday, before the new academic year begins, I promise to meet you and tell you my impressions. I'll find your phone number in your file."

He saw her to the door. Anna dashed outside, totally oblivious to the other students' presence. Her feet had grown wings. The weather was so nice that day. She felt like her life had suddenly got much prettier. She walked in the street, flashing her broadest smile at the passersby; she didn't care what they would think of her. She didn't want to do anything else for the day. She felt the need to kiss everyone she saw. She took off her jacket, rolled up her sleeves, and stepped into a cafe bar to ask for a glass of water as her mouth had gone dry. She didn't want to go back home, as she usually did. Without realising it, she entered a restaurant. She wanted to buy herself a meal as if celebrating something.

For the first time at this tender age, she felt like she was no longer alone. Like someone was sitting across the table and, without touching her food, she was staring deep into their eyes, travelling inside of them. The waiter's voice brought her back to reality with a bump:

"Are you dining alone, miss?"

"No, there's another one…er…sorry…just me…"

She went back home quite early. She didn't care what her mother would say. She was sure a new life was ahead of her. Intuition? Perhaps. She didn't even care if she would go on holiday this year. She wanted this summer to be as short as possible.

"Where have you been, my love? I was really worried! What took you so long?"

"I'm here, mum. I'm alright. Well, since today was the last day of the term, Emma and I thought we'd walk a little. We also had something to eat—you know, we had a chat and lost track of time. That's all!"

"Alright, my dear Anna! It's just that you've never been so late, so it's only natural that I grew worried."

Anna threw herself into her arms and, giving her a tight hug; she said how happy she was. Her mother looked at her and asked her with a knowing smile:

"Let me look at you. Your face is radiant! What's the matter, sweetheart?"

"Nothing special. It's just that the academic year is over and I've excelled myself, as Adolf told me...I mean the Professor of Philosophy..."

"That handsome man who speaks so beautifully?" asked Mrs. Bird.

Unable to hide a slight blush, Anna averted her eyes and simply nodded her head somewhat awkwardly.

Mrs. Bird smilingly kissed her and said:

"Go get some rest, love. We have a whole summer ahead of us to talk. You've grown up, my dear Anna..."

The next day, the moment she woke up, she called Emma. She wanted to check if she had seen her walk into Adolf's office so as to come up with a plausible excuse.

"Morning, girl! How are you? Sorry about yesterday. You know, I left in a hurry. Well, I...couldn't help myself! You see what I mean. Sorry about that, eh?"

"It's alright, Anna. There's no reason to apologise. Obviously, that's what happened."

"You're right. Then, I saw some classmates talking to the professor outside his office, so I mingled and lost track of time."

"Alright, I got it. Let's forget about all this...What are your plans for today? Shall we go shopping?"

"I don't know. Maybe. I'll call you later."

Deep down, Anna wanted to see her good friend, have a chat, laugh, and have fun. She felt like her heart had suddenly opened up; something urged her to get out and share her secret with the whole world. First of all, with Emma.

"No, it's still soon. After all, nothing's for sure and I don't want to jump to conclusions. Actually, he showed nothing more than a little fondness for me. I should keep my wits about me and be serious," she thought.

Two hours later, she enjoyed a hot coffee cup with Emma at a bar opposite the central square. Emma couldn't help, but notice how happy she was.

"What's the matter, girl? I see something special in your sparkling eyes. Will you tell me?"

"Nothing special. It's just that I'm happy this year's over. That's all…"

"You're sure? I think something else is going on. Something's sneaked into your heart, torturing you pleasantly," Emma said tongue-in-cheek.

Slightly blushing, Anna tried to avoid a reply, but she couldn't make it.

"Yes, I can't hide from you. There is something, but it's still soon. Yet, I want to assure you that you'll be the first one to know."

"I can wait. I'm not gonna push you if you don't want to tell me. Is it a classmate of ours?"

"No, no, I can't tell you anything right now. So shall we go window shopping?"

"Let's go. I'm waiting for you to tell me, although I think I've already realised what's going on."

CHAPTER FOUR

The following days were calm and uneventful for Anna. Her mother was happy to see her in high spirits, although her daughter's absentmindedness and agitation couldn't strike her at times. She repeatedly tried to talk to her about all this and find out what was going on. Mothers always care and are curious to know.

When she was at home, Anna spent most of her time in the office by the library. Although she was supposed to get some rest during the summer, she preferred to pore over the books for Adolf's modules.

Deep down, she wanted to spend her summer in the company of her professor— even through her Philosophy books. After a few days, her mother asked her about their vacations.

"This year, we must celebrate your success as a university student, and you need to rest, honey. Where do you want to go?"

She didn't expect such a reply.

"My sweet mummy, if you don't mind, I think I'll stay at home for the summer. After all, it's warm and I'm in no mood. I'd better rest here."

Mrs. Bird went closer, took her hand in her palm, and looked her in the eyes before saying:

"But you have to rest, darling. Is there a particular reason why you want to stay here?"

"No, no. It's exactly what I told you. I think it's better to rest here."

After a short pause, Anna asked:

"Mum, in Philosophy, we're taught about some very important ancient writers and poets who lived in a small country in the Mediterranean Sea called Greece. Do you know this country? I've heard it's really beautiful!"

Mrs. Bird seemed to get upset upon hearing this question, but she regained her composure within split seconds.

"Yes, I've heard of it, but who told you about all this? Your professor?"

"Of course! Who else? That's the core of his teaching, but I think you got upset, mum. Am I wrong?"

"Ah, no…I didn't get upset at all. It's just that…I'm struck by the fact that you often refer to your favourite professor, this Adolf, who's also handsome…"

"What are you talking about? How could you imagine there could be something going on between him and me? He just spoke the world of this place, and that he'll be holidaying there this year. That's why I asked you," Anna answered irritatedly and stood up.

"Alright, alright! Don't cut up rough! This place is too far away and, besides, it's way too expensive! Let's not carry on with this discussion. And make sure you don't let others affect you. We're going to spend the summer wherever, however, you like, but please don't bring up this subject again."

"You know, as my mind's travelling there, to this beautiful country that, according to Adolf, is very hot in the summer, and its beaches are fantastic, I want you to promise me that we're going to go there at some point in the future. You promise?" Anna asked again, her eyes shining with determination, which enraged Mrs. Bird for the first time.

"I said, end of discussion! We're not going to talk about this ever again!"

July found Anna alone. Emma had left for her summer vacations with her family. Irritated by her mother's reaction, she decided to stay in for the whole period. Her mind was stuck to him, and she felt resentful as they couldn't be together. She spent all her day poring over her books, especially her favourite 'Medea.' She started making up scenarios, although she didn't really care whether they would materialise. When the weather was good, she went out for a walk in the park, her only company being her thoughts and the new world she made up in her mind, feeling no guilt.

Yet, she hadn't made it clear what she was feeling exactly. If that's what love was like, then she was the happiest woman in the world. Her heart told her she wasn't wrong. The dream she was living would open up like a bud that spreads its leaves to embrace the sun's warm smile.

It was mid-August. That morning, Anna could barely get out of bed. She was off colour, and she barely touched her breakfast. She went to her office and tried to read something, hoping to shake off that strange burden she felt. All of a sudden, the phone shattered the silence. Instinctively, she sprung off her seat to answer it, but her mother was quicker.

"Hello? Who is this, please? Hello?"

"Who is it, mother? Maybe it's Emma. We're going out today."

"I don't know, my child. They hung up. They must have dialled the wrong number."

After a while, the phone rang again, and Anna picked it up as she was right next to it.

"Hi, girlie! How are you doing?"

"Morning, Emma! I'm doing great! Was it you who called a moment ago?"

"No, this is my first call," answered Emma.

Anna suddenly felt relieved, but she couldn't explain the reason. She got dressed, said goodbye to her mother, and went out. That morning, she didn't feel well and while Emma was talking to her about her holiday, Anna's mind was stuck to that phone call. Her intuition led her to him…

Late in the afternoon, when she got back home, the first thing she asked her mother was whether anyone had called—much to Mrs. Bird's surprise, who didn't even bother to answer this question. Anna went up to her room, but this time her mother followed suit. She wanted to tell her that the phone had rung again and they had hung up. Upon hearing this, Anna's heart started pounding.

"It must have been him. They can't have dialled the wrong number. If it was him, I'm sure he's on holiday and wants to talk to me. Am I overreacting?" she thought to herself. "I guess I'm being carried away by my emotions. Why would he ever call me? Just because we had a chat when we were left alone? Let's forget about all this."

After an entire week, no one ever called again. August was drawing to a close, and Anna had completely forgotten about all this when one morning while Mrs. Bird was out shopping, she suddenly heard the phone ring. As if someone else might pick it up, Anna rushed to answer it.

"Good morning. I'd like to speak to Anna, please."

"Speaking. Who is it?"

"My dear Anna, good morning. I recognised your voice this time, but I just wanted to make sure. It's Adolf. Can I speak freely?"

Her heart missed a beat.

"Professor, I don't know what to say…," Anna faltered.

"Sorry to disturb you. Can I talk to you?"

"Yes, sure! My mother's out. Don't hang up this time. Well…I didn't expect it…I mean, I did expect your phone call…What am I saying? Please forgive me. I'm at a loss for words."

"Please take it easy. I just called as I promised. I'll tell you about my trip and holiday. I called several times, but obviously, it was your mother who answered, so I hung up."

Anna didn't have the time to reply. She only wanted to listen to him before her mother came back home.

"Anna, do you hear me?"

"Yes, yes, go ahead."

"I'd love to talk to you about this experience for hours on end, but I'll tell you in a hurry that I spent a most unforgettable summer, a very warm summer. There, everyone is on the beach, enjoying themselves. Also, the food is very delicious, and the people so hospitable. Maybe I should stop, eh?"

"Please carry on," Anna said on the spot, plunged into her dream. She feared she might wake up.

"Well, as I said, everything was so perfect there. My friend and peer showed me around the museums and theatres under the Acropolis with the renowned Parthenon. Of course, one night with a full moon, at the Ancient Theatre of Epidaurus, I enjoyed an ancient comedy by a great poet, Aristophanes. The thing is—please allow me to say that Anna—, I felt kind of lonely. I felt like that on other occasions too, but this time my feeling of solitude was deeper. Still, this has been a problem for years now."

"Please, don't stop." Anna had already got over the initial shock.

"Well…what I mean is that you enjoy life in a different way when you can share your joy with someone else. I won't weary you anymore. I felt the need to open up my heart to someone and I thought of you—please, don't take offence! I apologise for that…"

"No, no, you made me really happy by calling me," replied Anna, without even realising it, had already dispensed with formalities. "I spent a most tedious summer. I didn't want to go on holiday, although my mother insisted. I stayed at home, hung around with my friend Emma, and all I did every day was leaf through next year's books!"

"Why? That was wrong! You should have got some rest. After all, that 'Medea' you obsessed over tackles an extremely heavy topic, and it's not a summer read. Alright, I'll offer you private tuition!" Adolf said with a laugh. 'I'd better hang up now. I've tired you out. It was nice talking to you. See you soon in the amphitheatre, in less than a month. I want to see you in your seat, as always."

"Adolf, this phone call has been the greatest joy in my life so far. The whole room radiates with this joy! Farewell! I promise to be there in the same seat, right opposite your podium."

That was it. Now she believed that all her dreams would come true. She needn't dream anymore as she was literally living all her fantasies.

"He called me! I'll lose my mind! All this is nothing, but a big truth…" She was so overjoyed that she started pacing up and down the living room. She barely heard her surprised mother, who was standing in front of her. Without any inhibitions, Anna threw herself into her arms and began kissing her. She didn't realise what she was doing exactly. Mrs. Bird's intuition, though—her motherly intuition, that is—, was infallible.

"Now I'm sure, love that you're smitten, although you're still so young…"

"Yes, mum, that's what's probably happening to me." Her face lit up with joy.

"Are you going to tell me? It must be a classmate of yours, right?"

"Yes, yes, from the uni, but please forgive me as I can't tell you anything yet. It's too soon and I'm scared. Anyway, you're going to be the first to know, I promise."

Happy as a lark seeing her only daughter in high spirits, Mrs. Bird bent over and planted a kiss on her cheek.

"My dear Anna, if your father were alive, he'd be so happy!" she told her as she went up the stairs, trying to hide a tear that ran down her cheek.

Anna was sure of Adolf's feelings. What she felt was so strong that she didn't want to think about his position, their age difference, or even her own place in society. Everything inside of her had radically changed. She felt she had grown up overnight.

As she plunged into her own world and thoughts, she began to make plans for the remainder of the summer. She felt that love, this wonderful emotion that overwhelmed her heart and soul, had put wings on her feet. She had even forgotten about her studies. Books played second fiddle.

CHAPTER FIVE

Every day drags for Anna. The rough patch she went through during the summer is gone, and now she can't wait to get back to the amphitheatre, and take her seat opposite Adolf.

The weather changes, gradually getting colder; still, Anna's heart is warm, keeping summer's heat inside her. She has to wake up early tomorrow morning. After saying goodnight to her mother, she pleads with her to wake her up on time, and Mrs. Bird smilingly promises to do so.

"I feel so happy that you are in high spirits. That's how I want you to feel from now on: happy and lucky. Be careful, though, as life also holds sorrow in store. You're still young and guileless. I'll stand by you as a mother and friend; that's why I want you to share your worries and problems with me, darling."

"Alright, mum. You know how much I love you and I promise you'll be the first one I'll talk to. After all, you are the only person I have in life."

The next day, she did everything in a hurry. She couldn't wait to leave. She nibbled her breakfast, kissed her mother goodbye, and in ten minutes boarded the bus. Her eyes through the blurry window saw the passersby hurrying to work, their faces sullen. For Anna, though, they all looked happy because that's how she felt. She met Emma outside her Faculty.

"Morning, girlie. Here we are again! Let me take a closer look at you. You're dressed to kill! Something good must have happened to you during the summer—I can see it on your face."

"Come on! What are you talking about? Nothing happened. When would it ever happen as we met twenty days ago?" Anna replied spontaneously and pulled her by the hand to enter the amphitheatre, fearing she would let the cat out of the bag.

"You can't wait, eh? It's still early for the lecture. Come sit here for a chat."

But Anna had already walked into the amphitheatre, her eyes falling there, on the second row, to check if her seat was available. Although the amphitheatre was almost empty, Anna ran to take her seat; then, she signalled to her friend to sit beside her. In a while, the students' voices resounded throughout the hall. Anna felt somewhat nervous, but she had a hunch that the door would open in a while, and Adolf—no one else—would show up. She felt everyone's glances searing her, which made her feel awkward. "That's so silly of me," she said to herself and looked back to see if all this was true.

"Good morning, my dear students. Welcome to our new academic year. I welcome you on behalf of the other professors and wish you…"

As if struck by lightning, Anna abruptly turned to look ahead. It was his voice.

"I hope you make progress this year as well."

He stood there, right in front of her, looking serious and handsome in his dark suit. He was gorgeous! While he was speaking, Anna unwittingly fixed her eyes on him, which didn't escape Emma's notice. At some point, her friend brought her back to reality by nudging her.

"What are you staring at him for? It's not the first time you've seen him!"

Anna didn't reply as she was lost in her own world. She seemed to be oblivious to everything around her. Adolf didn't look at her, but she couldn't care less. It was more than enough for her to see and listen to him. She didn't want to think that what had happened in the summer was just a figment of her imagination.

The permanent smile across her face stayed there for the whole day, even when he left the amphitheatre. The rest of the day was indifferent.

"Will you tell me what's going on?" Emma asked persistently as they walked to the bus station.

"Emma, my beloved friend, something's happening to me, something really good, but for the time being, I don't want to talk to anyone about it. When I'm ready, you'll be the first one to know."

"What if I've already realised what's happening?"

"Then, please be patient if you love me. Not even I know exactly what's going on with me. I'm afraid and I need a little more time. Maybe I'm wrong. I love you so much!" Anna replied hastily and got on the bus, which had already arrived.

Nothing changed over the following days. No call, no sign, no change in Adolf's behaviour. Anna felt disillusioned and plunged into her thoughts once again, cooped up in her room.

"Am I wrong? Maybe he simply likes me. Maybe all this was because I excelled at school, but my feelings are real. Perhaps I mistake my own feelings for his. I'm just a nineteen-year-old university student. He's much older and my professor. Yes, but why did he call me in the summer just after he returned from his holiday? Why did he call me and not Emma or someone else? I can't be that wrong! My heart can't fail me!"

Impatient at this tender age, Anna got more nervous and absentminded and began to lag behind with her studies. She avoided her mother and Emma and kept herself to herself, lost in her own world for hours on end.

It was December, Christmas was just around the corner, and the School would break up for a few days. For almost a week, Anna had been bedridden, running a fever. The flu rampant in Europe had darkened her door. Mrs. Bird never left her side. The family doctor reassured her that everything would be fine and recommended that Anna should not get out of bed or go out, and make sure to take her medicine.

But Anna was not only sick; she was hurt as well. She kept complaining that she didn't want to stay in bed anymore, and she couldn't wait to go back to her School. Her mother told her that her health was more important.

That afternoon, sad as she was, Anna heard the phone ring. She hopped out of bed and ran down the stairs. Her mother wasn't at home. Her heart almost leapt out of her chest until she answered it. She had a hunch.

"Could I speak to Miss Anna, please?"

"Speaking…"

"My dear Anna, it's me, Adolf. Can I speak to you?"

"Yes, sure! My mother's not here."

"You know, I was really worried. You've missed so many classes. Of course, I know many students have come down with the flu, but…well…I was really worried about you. Are you alright?"

Suddenly, as if taking heart, Anna stood on her two feet.

"Thanks a lot for your interest, professor…er…I mean Adolf. The truth is, I was really weak when the flu struck me, but I'm better now."

"You mean your situation was serious? I want to know. Are you feverish?"

"Yes, I ran a high fever, but now it's gone down. Thanks once again. Although I was burning, my mind was there, in the second row. Have I missed out on important things?" asked Anna with a laugh.

"No, I did some revisions due to the situation. After all, very few students attended. A very good student was also missing. You know, she excelled herself last year, so interest flagged," Adolf said, laughing out loud as well.

"You know, my mother was really sad and asked me not to attend until the Christmas holiday so that I'll have completely recovered for the new year."

"She's right."

"Yes, but I want to come tomorrow morning."

"Why are you in such a hurry?"

"Well…you know…I'm afraid someone else will take my seat."

"Is this the reason?"

"Er…there's another one, a more serious reason, but it's my secret, and I don't want to share it with anyone."

"Not even with me? Not as your professor, of course, but let's say I'm a good friend of yours."

"A friend? But…I don't see you only as a friend," Anna replied self-assuredly.

"My sweet Anna, let's put an end to this conversation over the phone. We have so much time ahead to talk. I promise to see you by New Year's Eve—if you're up and about, that is. I want to talk to you, to tell you about my wonderful holiday."

"Alright, I'll be as right as rain tomorrow," Anna said spontaneously, making Adolf laugh out loud.

When Mrs. Bird returned home, she found her daughter lying on the sofa in the living room, reading a book.

"Why have you got up, my love? You're still weak."

"I feel great, mum," she answered, her eyes lighting up with joy.

"Did anything happen while I was away? Your face radiates, and I'm so glad about that. Let me check if you have a fever."

"I'm fine, I tell ya! I'm thinking of going out tomorrow."

"You must be kidding! We said you're going back to school after the Christmas holidays."

But Anna didn't care about that. She had been living her dream for the past hour or so. Everything was real. "He's so serious. I'm the one who can't wait. I shouldn't be so frivolous. From now on, I'm going to do what Adolf tells me," she murmured so that her mum wouldn't hear, and went to her room.

She felt rejuvenated after a week. She gradually started to eat, and her mother promised to visit her aunt, her father's sister, who invited them to celebrate New Year's Day together. They didn't get on very well, but Mrs. Bird saw that as an opportunity for Anna to get out after so long. Ever since her husband Hans died, Anna's mother didn't want to visit his parents very often as they all, including Hans, served Germany's previous regime, which she didn't like at all. However, as she had married Hans years earlier and really loved him, she didn't pay attention to all this. After all, from 1937 to the day he died in 1945, Hans served as an ambassador in many countries.

CHAPTER SIX

On New Year's Day, everything was covered in snow, but the roads were free—as always. Germany's rapid economic growth, mainly that of Berlin in the western part of the once beautiful capital city, was visible across the board—preponderantly in its citizens' standard of living.

Aunt Eda welcomed the two women most cordially. She hadn't seen Anna for more than a couple of years, that's why the young girl was the first one she hugged. She always called her 'little Anna.' Then, she hugged Mrs. Bird.

"Welcome home! Happy New Year! Welcome, my beauty! Oh, my sweet girl, you've grown up and you're a wild beauty! Come on in. Take a seat."

"Good morning, Aunt Eda. I see you're just fine. What with the uni, which is so time-consuming, I don't have much free time," said Anna, and her mother hastened to nod her head.

"I understand, my love. You should know how happy I was to learn you were admitted to the uni. Your father would be really proud if he were with us. He'd also be proud of your beauty too. Bird, I'm afraid you're going to lose her soon. Be careful as someone may take her away from you," said aunt Eda laughingly, making Anna blush.

"Thank you for your kind words, Eda, but she's still too young for all that. Her studies come first," Mrs. Bird answered contentedly.

Eda had always been a gossip. She didn't have a family, and Anna's mother always felt she was jealous of her. At lunchtime, aunt Eda made sure to refer to Anna's father—he was her brother—, who had an early death; he died when Anna was two years old. While Eda was talking about her brother and Anna's childhood, Mrs. Bird felt irritated, that's why she tried to change the subject. She didn't want to talk about Hans very much, which was exactly what she avoided discussing with her daughter as well. Still, they had a good time. Anna's high spirits had also played a role—but she had her own reasons. Late in the evening, they went back home. New Year's Day had drawn to a close. At least that's what she felt.

In a few days, School opened up, and Anna was up and about after such a long time. She was strong and ready for the new year's challenges. What had mainly changed, though, inside her soul was that she felt much more confident. She started studying her books again with more determination this year. She wanted to make up for all the wasted time and become even better. She wanted to be a top student so as to make him happy. Now it dawned on her that Adolf's seriousness and aloofness meant to protect her as well as himself. She felt secure and sure of his feelings. She was certain that Adolf would overcome all the problems that kept them apart. She started having dreams about the years to come, and she was over the moon.

"Is this what love and bliss are like?" she wondered. She mulled over these two words all the time, night and day. She went so far as to imagine living with him, and sometimes her mind stopped there as if a kind of fear stood in the way. She had to wait. It was also Mrs. Bird, who would surely raise objections. Still, she knew that her mother loved her and wouldn't stop her from fulfilling her dreams. She was sure she would talk her into it.

This winter wasn't heavy. Every single morning, Anna was there, in the second row, opposite the podium. She was opposite that man who would conquer her heart and life, as it seemed.

Today, Adolf seemed a little absentminded during his lecture. Anna was focusing on him rather than the lesson; maybe she was the cause of his absentmindedness. When the lecture drew close, Adolf told her to drop by his office without caring if other people were watching. Anna was taken by storm while Emma was even more astonished.

"Is something the matter, girl? What does he want to tell you in private?"

"I don't know. Let's wait and see. Maybe something about the module," Anna was quick to respond and stood up. In three minutes, she stepped into his office. Formal and serious, Adolf asked her to sit down and apologised to her for being so absentminded during the lecture.

"My dear Anna, I only have ten minutes. This is not the right place to tell you what I've meant to share with you all this time. Don't get me wrong. I know very well that I'm in a difficult position, just like you are. I just happened to muster up the courage to talk to you today, not as a professor, but as Adolf."

Anna felt her heart was going to leap out of her chest. She stood still staring at him.

"Go on," she urged him.

But time was up already. Feeling awkward and apprehensive, Adolf stood up and held her hand.

"There's so much I need to tell you that it's going to take me hours, and it's so stifling in here. I promise to see you off-campus and tell you what I haven't been able to tell you today."

He sounded so determined that Anna couldn't ask for clarifications. She only nodded her head, held his hand, and ran out of the office. All she managed to do before she opened the door was to falter: "I'll be waiting for as long as is necessary…I'll be waiting…"

Walking out of the room, she stumbled upon Emma in the corridor, who was waiting for her with bated breath. Anna, who no longer wanted to share her secret with anyone else, cut her in:

"You know, it wasn't anything serious. He just wanted to tell me that I should work harder as I've lagged behind and I won't have the same performance as last year…"

"Is that all or is something going on? This is the third time he's asked to see you in his office. Don't you need some help from your best friend? Something's pestering you," Emma told her knowingly.

"What are you talking about, girl? He's a very serious man! How on earth did you think of such a thing?" Anna asked her brusquely and took her by the hand to enter the next class.

Winter months passed quickly, and Anna was in a hurry. She had a hunch that the following summer would be the best. She wanted to be his best student—and not only that.

And she made it in June's exam period.

On the last day of the academic year, the amphitheatre was packed, and Anna was in her seat, as always. Adolf was on the podium. They exchanged the same wishes. She felt like rising from her seat, hugging him, and wishing him in person, or rather asking him to holiday together this summer, so that he wouldn't feel lonely anymore. She wanted to tell him that she didn't want to spend the summer on her own. She'd love to make everyone go away so that their lips would say what they had left unspoken that day in his office. She longed to be with him night and day throughout the summer, looking at him and listening attentively…

Without realising it, she had stayed in her seat. Everyone else was gone. Emma wasn't beside her. She hadn't attended, due to a family problem. Looking around her, Anna snapped out of her reverie and walked away too.

"Still, within a few minutes, I read all those beautiful thoughts that flashed through your mind."

Anna was startled by Adolf's voice.

"What are you? A magician?" she asked him smilingly.

"Let's take a walk," he suggested and she was all too happy to agree. The weather was quite mild so that they could stroll in the park.

"I won't tell you about my holiday this time. I'm staying here this year. What about you?"

"Then, I'm staying here too. I mean, I'm staying here again," Anna said knowingly.

"I promised to tell you a lot as I feel the need to share them with you, but I'll let you go home now because they might see us and it's not appropriate. I'll give you my phone number as I live on my own. I mean, not exactly. An old lady that does the house chores lives with me as well. She's been working with us ever since I was little. I'm like her son. You see, I was an only child. You call me as it's kind of hard for me because of your mother. Don't you worry about anything; you're always on my mind. I have so much to tell you. Before you call me, though, make sure you speak to yourself and your heart as you're still young."

"I feel old enough and I think I'm quite mature, especially over the last year," Anna hastened to reply, clutching the piece of paper his phone number was written on. She held his hand, looking him in the eyes. She felt the need to kiss him, but she restrained herself. He wouldn't want such a thing.

As she left, she felt she was flying. She didn't even look back to see him go away as she feared all this was a lie or a dream. Boarding the bus, she opened her sweaty palm and read his phone number again and again.

"I'd better learn it by heart," she thought to herself.

As soon as she opened her house door, she ran to her room. She didn't even notice that her mother seemed to be sleeping on the sofa in the living room. She lay in bed and tried to put her thoughts in order. So much had happened to her over the last year. For the first time today, she felt what Eros and Love are like. Everything was such a tangle inside of her...

"I have to talk to my mother," she thought. "She's the only person who really loves me, but will she understand? The age difference, the studies..." She shot to her feet, changed clothes, and went downstairs.

"No, I mustn't tell her anything. It's so soon. After all, Adolf and I haven't talked yet, and I don't know what exactly he's going to tell me. I guess I'm in a hurry. He's older and more experienced, so he knows what I should do." She felt that, although everything had happened so fast, she had to trust him blindly. That's exactly what she was going to do.

CHAPTER SEVEN

Day by day, the weather was looking up as the summer had made its appearance. Anna was ready to see him. Some phobias that sneaked into her soul, making her feel kind of insecure, were completely gone. That morning, she was in high spirits. As soon as her mother opened the door to go shopping, Anna, wasting no time, rushed to the phone. After all, she had learnt his phone number by heart.

"Hello? Who is it?" she heard his steady voice at the other end of the line.

"Good morning. It's me, Anna."

"Good morning, sweetheart. I think it took you some time to call me," he answered laughingly.

"No, no, I wanted to call you on the same day, but I hesitated. I didn't know how you'd take it."

"Well, today's a beautiful day. Shall we have our first secret date?"

"Sure! That's exactly what I meant to say," replied Anna in a confident, steady voice.

They were supposed to meet somewhere far away, in another area. Anna left a message for her mother, saying that she was going out with Emma and some other friends. After she got dressed and combed her hair in front of the mirror, she left with aplomb, ready to conquer her dream. It felt that way. She felt that was the beginning of her life. She believed that this life would give her all the joy and bliss a woman can find. In almost an hour, she stepped into a luxury cafe bar downtown.

He was there waiting for her. Self-assured as a mature woman, she crossed the long corridor and, before she even said 'good morning,' Adolf was already bolted upright, showing her to her seat. He was so gorgeous…

"Today stands before me the most beautiful woman in the world, and I feel so great! Today, my sweet Anna, you don't stand before the Professor of Philosophy in the amphitheatre, but you're with plain Adolf. I picked this cosy place as I have to tell you things about me and you, and I must add that I already feel awkward, as if this were the first time…"

Anna smiled, oozing confidence, and returned the compliment.

"Well, before me stands not the aloof, serious, and strict Professor of Philosophy, but a handsome man, the most handsome man in the world," she said, making him beam at her.

After ordering their drinks, they broke the ice completely. They began to talk about their families. Adolf talked to her about his parents. He had lost them both in the bombings at the end of the horrible war. His father was a high-ranking officer serving the Nazi regime and wanted his son to pursue the same profession. Adolf seemed to be irritated by Anna's 'why?', but after hesitating for a few seconds, he told her that his dream was to study and pursue an academic career.

When it was Anna's turn to talk about her parents, she mentioned her father first, who died of a heart attack when she was only two, so she had no recollection of him. She told him he was a diplomat, a high-ranking employee of the Ministry of Foreign Affairs, with the same regime Adolf's father served.

"My mother," continued Anna, "according to what she told me later, when I grew up, never agreed with my father's obsession with Nazism. After all, after he died, that was the reason why she avoided seeing his sister, who is still alive and kicking."

Seemingly rankled by their conversation, which touched upon their insipid past, he reached out to hold her hand tenderly for the first time.

"All these sad things belong to the past, sweetheart. Life lies ahead, and that's how we should see it—both of us. This country we live in is trying to forget and shake off its guilty past, and we have to follow its example. After my parents were gone, I lived with my grandparents for many years, as I told you. I was at a tender age back then. Still, I wasn't so little as not to remember that hell."

"What do you mean?" wondered Anna, holding his hand tight.

"Ah…no…er…I mean the war, the bombings," Adolf answered as if dazed for a few seconds. "Let's not discuss all this. It's my fault. Let's leave all this behind. Let's talk about us. Well, my dear Anna, I'll talk to you straight out. For the past year, I've felt in love with a beautiful young lady. She's so pretty that she reminds me of an exquisite goddess—I cannot, but refer to Greek Mythology again!—, named Venus. Do you mind my calling you like this sometimes?"

Anna's hands went numb. She couldn't utter a single word. She was still looking him in the eyes, her hands clasping his. After a while, she felt confident enough to speak. She told him about her feelings for him, how much she admired him, how happy she was, and what dreams she had.

They went out, walked around the park for a while, with Anna clinging her body to him. For the first time, Adolf bent over and kissed her, bringing her closer to his body. Looking deep into her eyes, he asked her to marry him.

"Sweetheart, as I don't want all this to take us ages, and I would like to see how your mother reacts, I propose to you and, if you say 'yes,' I'll come over to your place to see her.

"I'm one hundred percent sure of my feelings, and I want to assure you that they are real. I also want to tell you that it took me some time to raise a family, but now I want to carry on with my life by your side to the bitter end. I understand that I may put you in a difficult position right now, but I can't wait any longer. First of all, you have to give it some serious thought and talk to your mother. You're still young and maybe she won't agree. I'll be waiting for your reply, whether you say yes or no."

"My reply is a big 'YES'! No one else, but you lives in my dreams. I don't know if what I feel is love but, if it's true, then I'm the happiest woman in the world, and I want to marry the man who's holding me in his arms so tenderly right now—no one else! I also want to swear to you that I'll be by your side to the bitter end."

After holding her tight for a few minutes, Adolf told her to keep their relationship under wraps until it was made official.

"After a few days, my dear Anna, you can tell your mother, and I will visit her straight away."

"You've already made me the happiest woman on Earth! I'll speak to strict Mrs. Bird tomorrow, and rest assured that, even if she raises objections, I will talk her into it in the end. She loves me too much to deny me this bliss."

She stole a kiss from him and ran to the bus stop.

Anna's life had a meaning. She was suddenly overwhelmed with all these unprecedented feelings. She felt no fear. She didn't even consider the slightest reaction on her mother's part. She didn't care whether she was too young for him. All she could see was him. She didn't want to wake up from that dream, lest it not be real. She wanted to speak to Mrs. Bird immediately. How would she take it, though? Probably not very well. She had figured out that something was wrong, but she would never think of Adolf. Anna couldn't wait to tell her the truth.

Walking in, she spontaneously ran to hug her mother.

"I love you so much, mum! Tell me if you love me back too!"

"What kind of question is that, honey? Sure I love you! You're my whole life. Let me look at you…," said Mrs. Bird, after giving her a light push to take a closer look at her. "You're radiant! Is there something you want to tell me? You shouldn't keep secrets from me. We've lived together for so long, and we're not supposed to hide things. Isn't that so, my dear? I never hid anything from you. I've always been honest. That's what I want you to be."

That very moment, Anna felt like a cold gust of air swept through her body through her beloved mother's warm hands. An indeterminate kind of fear gripped her.

Mrs. Bird instantly realised that and before she had the time to ask her what was going on, Anna mustered up the courage to talk to her.

"You know, mum, you said we shouldn't keep secrets from each other, so…I want to share my own secret with you. It makes me so happy, but I don't know how you're going to take it."

Upset by this conversation, Mrs. Bird pulled her daughter closer to her on the big sofa, taking on her strict expression; she asked her what was going on. She seemed to be afraid of what she would hear. Anna took a deep breath and, plucking up courage; she started telling her about her own story in a steady voice:

"Mum, I don't know what you'll say and how you're going to take this, but what you'll hear is a big truth for me now and for the rest of my life. As you've already realised, something has changed in my life for the past few months. I'm in love with a charming man, and he loves me too!"

"I've figured it all out, my dear. All mothers instantly understand such things. What strikes me as odd is this 'charming man' you said. Isn't he one of your classmates or friends at the university?"

"No, mum. He's not my age or one of my friends. After all, I only hang out with Emma. He's outside the University."

They were both in uncharted waters now. Mrs. Bird leapt to her feet and nervously took a few steps. Anna, undaunted and confident, continued:

"As I don't want to tire you, mum, I'll talk to you straight out. I love so much and want to live my life with my Professor of Philosophy, Mr. Adolf Krause. I've told you about him before. He loves me too and wants to come over to speak to you. He doesn't want to keep our affair under wraps anymore."

Keeping her wits about her, her mother went closer, sat beside her, stroked her head, and said in a calm voice:

"My dear child, I didn't realise when you grew up… no one can stop this love that visited your heart and made it leap with joy. I'm so happy for you! Of course, I never expected to hear all this. Still, my sweetheart, he's really old for you. You're still young and…well…I don't know anything about him and his family. Maybe it's rash of you…"

Anna felt relaxed. Her mother's first reaction was really positive. She threw herself into her arms.

"No, no, there's no obstacle. If you love me so much, please don't say no if you really love me, don't say no. This is the first time I've ever felt so happy! He's serious, single, and lives on his own. His parents were killed in the bombings. He is a self-made man and so… handsome! You'll see, you're going to like him on the spot! As for his age, I don't care at all. He's 38 and, when he speaks to me, I feel so secure! Please, mummy, don't say no. He wants to meet you and talk to you.

"That's my secret. I told you on the spot. I didn't keep it to myself or date him on the sly. He doesn't want that either. Didn't you tell me you don't keep secrets from me?"

As if struck by lightning, Mrs. Bird sprung up from the couch and replied:

"Alright, honey, alright. Sorry I'm a little bit upset, but…well, I'm a mother and all this came as a shock. Maybe I don't want to lose you so early; maybe I'm afraid I'm going to end up alone. My dear, you're still so young and…I'm scared. Anyway, all of a sudden, today I saw a grownup woman before my eyes. You've grown up so fast, my daughter. When you were only two months and I held you in my arms, I never thought this day would come."

"Why did you say 'two months' and not the moment I was born?"

"Oh, I don't know what came over me…Ah, yes, you were so weak and tiny that your dad and I were afraid to hold you. He didn't want to do it until you gained some weight. He was so scared!" said Mrs. Bird smilingly, then she bent over to kiss her. "Yes, baby, you're right. I guess your heart is right. Tell Adolf I'll be glad to talk to him, but you should know I haven't given my consent yet."

After dancing in the living room, Anna leapt to her feet and threw herself into her mother's arms again.

"You make me so happy! For the second time today, I feel on top of the world. Thank you so much!"

That night, Anna didn't sleep a wink. She couldn't believe that she could live her dream from that day on. All night, she was trying to realise if what she felt was passion, love, or something else that she couldn't explain. No matter what it was, though, it was beautiful. She stayed still in bed till dawn. She waited for the sun to rise to tell him to visit them as soon as he could, in case something changed.

Although she hadn't slept at all in the morning, Anna had breakfast well-rested and in high spirits, which couldn't go unnoticed.

"Morning, mummy! I want you to know that you made me so happy yesterday."

"Morning, honey! You're so radiant! Last night, I mulled over what we discussed. Above all, I'm interested to see you happy and, before you make up your mind, I want you to give yourself some time. I like it that you didn't hide it from me and, if you're really sure about it, you can tell Adolf to come over to get to know each other and talk. I want to believe that

I will like him and…probably…I will give you my blessing. But, first, I want you to be one hundred percent sure before you decide."

"Mum, I've already made my decision. You'll see, he's a wonderful person, and I'll tell you something I didn't mention yesterday. I've found out that the only thing he's interested in is his science. That's what he's devoted his whole life to. He's not gossip, he takes no interest in politics, and he's not concerned with the past. Of course, besides his job, he's also going to take care of me," answered Anna with a broad smile.

As soon as she was done with her breakfast, she stayed in the office to relax and read a book. It was the one left open from last year. 'Medea' a formidable ancient tragedy with a terrible ending. It was Adolf's favourite play, whose staggering plot and theme had influenced Anna as well. The following year, she longed to hear Adolf himself analyse it and answer all her queries. From now on, she would have him all to herself for the rest of her life. He would talk to her about all this and much more.

While her mind was travelling across the pages of the book, her eyes were stuck on the clock on the wall. At around eleven, she went up to her room and, in a while, after she repeated his phone number over and over again, she went downstairs.

He answered her phone call immediately as if he were expecting it.

"Good morning, my dear…"

Before he completed his phrase, Anna interrupted him to announce the good news.

"Let me tell you! My mother gave her consent. Do you want to know? Let me tell you now that she's out. It's really interesting. What d'you think?"

"Yes, I'm all ears, sweetheart," Adolf answered laughingly.

"Well…you know, she pushed me at first. I was scared, but I soon plucked up courage when she told me she had realised what was going on and a mother and a child shouldn't keep secrets. When she said all these years she had never hidden anything from me, I told her what I want to do in my life from now on."

"Take it easy! You'll choke!" Adolf told her. "Tell me calmly what exactly you talked about."

"My feelings for you and your feelings for me. At first, she was surprised; she was kind of negative; she told me about the age difference, saying I'm still very young. She asked me about you but, when I told her I'd never want to keep anything under wraps after she nervously paced up and down, she came closer, hugged me, and gave me her consent. When are you coming over? Today? Tomorrow at the latest!"

"Alright, alright, honey. Don't get all worked up! I want it to happen as soon as possible. Calm down. You want me to come over tomorrow?"

"Yes, yes, tomorrow. I'll tell her when she comes back. Tomorrow at noon. Please, promise me that you'll stay for lunch. It's homemade food. You should know that mum's an amazing cook!"

"We've got a deal, then! I promise I'll be with you to make you happy for the rest of our life."

Mrs. Bird too, wanted to see her daughter happy, that's why she went shopping the following morning. She would take care of their official guest as best as possible.

At noon, everything was ready, and they heard the doorbell.

"Good morning, Mrs. Meisner. If I'm not mistaken, you must be Anna's mother."

"Good morning, Professor. And you must be Adolf," Mrs. Bird answered with a broad smile of admiration. "Please, come in."

Behind Mrs. Bird, Anna, prettier than ever before, couldn't hide her joy. Adolf paid his respects with a gentleman's suaveness; in a few minutes, they had broken the ice. Anna's mother played an important role in that. Therefore, to liven up the atmosphere, she cut to the chase:

"Mr. Krause, can I call you Adolf?"

"Sure, Mrs. Bird. I've come here today for a holy cause. Of course, there must be some things that make you somewhat hesitant like our age difference, but I'd like to tell you that I'm not very old. I'm 38. I've lived on my own since 1945. My parents got killed in the city's bombings, and since then, I'd lived with my grandparents for almost a decade until they both passed away. I'm completely devoted to my science, and managed to be appointed as a Professor of Philosophy at the Department of Classics."

"What did your father do as a living?"

"He was a high-ranking military officer who served in various posts during the war."

"Did you do your military service?"

"Yes…but…you know, I avoid talking about that period as it only brought hardships to the world—and our own country, of course. Let's not dwell on this if you don't mind. I've left all this behind for years now, and today I'm here to talk to you about myself and Anna."

"You're right, my child; this war only brought calamities. I'll only say that Anna's father was a high-ranking officer of the Ministry of Foreign Affairs and, before our daughter was born, we had lived in many European countries. He was a nice man. He died of a heart attack in 1944 when Anna was only one and a half years old. She barely remembers him."

"So you were outside Germany in 1944?"

"Ah…no, no, we were here," Mrs. Bird replied somewhat awkwardly. "You see? We're talking about the past again! All these grim events are of no interest to anyone, let alone you and Anna. Let's talk about your future. I'll be frank with you, Adolf. For me, Anna's the most precious thing I have in life. Just like every mother, I would like her to find a man for the rest of her life. A nice man, someone to take care of her, respect her, and love her above all. She thinks the world of you but, to be honest, I can see that my only daughter has struck gold: she's found a nice, serious, and collected person. I also want you to know that you'll have a woman who will stand by you. I said 'woman,' although she's still young because I believe she will mature by your side."

While they were talking, Anna was watching silently, with a permanent smile across her lips that radiated with joy. She didn't want to interrupt their discussion as she thought she had to let her mother do the talking that day. Anna just wanted to look on…

As he wanted to end their discussion, Adolf expressed his true and deep feelings for Anna and promised to take care of and stand by her all his life. He would never make her feel sad.

A while later, Adolf sampled Mrs. Bird's cuisine and couldn't, but express his admiration. Today, life changed for him as well, not only for Anna. Besides their love, they would enjoy a comfortable life. He had inherited a huge fortune from his parents since he was their only child. His only relative was aunt Greta, his father's sister, whom he loved a lot and often visited. She was like a mother to him.

CHAPTER EIGHT

The summer of 1963 was different—for Anna, for Adolf, for the whole of Germany. Everyone knew that the country was split in two. Life on the western side was moving rapidly towards progress across the board. As if she had been born again, Anna lived her dream by Adolf's side and didn't want anyone to shatter it. In him, she saw what every girl her age dreamt of.

As neither Mrs. Bird nor Adolf wanted to delay the couple's wedding, they agreed to hold their official engagement at Anna's place in a few days, together with her best friend Emma, and aunt Greta, a kind educated old lady, who took to Anna from the word go.

So that summer was uneventful. Adolf didn't want to go on holiday. He asked Anna to stay in the city and visit its attractions together. After all, they had so much to share with each other and, above all, to discuss their wedding. Mrs. Bird looked so happy with this turn of events as she saw her only daughter in high spirits. Besides, she was sure that Adolf could secure her future. She had appreciated him as a serious, educated man and, every time she looked into his eyes, she saw real love for her daughter. She too wanted the wedding to take place as soon as possible, that's why she asked him to see to it, to which he agreed on the spot. Therefore, they set a date for early September, before the new academic year commenced.

The only issue now was whether Anna would continue her studies, but Adolf had already made up his mind about that. Therefore, one day they spent together, Adolf decided to talk to her, knowing that she would raise objections.

"Sweetheart, as your mother—justifiably so—wants the wedding to take place as soon as possible, to which I agree, I think we should hold it in early September. What do you think?"

"What can I say? You make me the happiest woman on earth! Surprises never stop with you!" Anna said and threw herself into his arms.

"But we must also discuss the issue of your studies. Tell me what you want. Will you continue or stay at home so that we'll raise a happy family since we both were unfortunate enough to be deprived of so many things?"

"I will do as you see fit," Anna whispered in his ear without giving it much thought. "Of course, I may not like it a lot, but…well…I think it's going to be hard for me to see before me in the amphitheatre not only my beloved professor, but also my beloved husband! I'll be feeling weird! The only sad thing is that someone else will take my seat in the second row," said Anna and burst into laughter.

Adolf threw his arms around her.

"Thank you, honey. That's how I see it and I want you to know that inside this empty house, which you will fill with your presence, you'll find another seat. When I'm with you—for the best part of the day—, I'll teach you much more."

That year, September was rainy and cold. Though, the black and grey clouds weren't capable of ruining Adolf and Anna's happiest moment. It was the beginning of a life they would spend together to the bitter end. Their wedding was attended by Mrs. Bird, Adolf's aunt, Emma, and a few other groom's friends.

Over the following hours, Anna stepped into her husband's beautiful neoclassical house as its new landlady. She would embark on a new life she had never thought of. She could barely imagine living absolute love from such an early age.

The new academic year began in a few days. However, this year Anna wouldn't be there in her favourite amphitheatre, in the second row. She would stay in her new home, away from her mother, but with the man, she loved and believed in. She wouldn't lose her best friend Emma, but see her only within the university's precincts. Emma had promised to be with her whenever she needed her. She was determined to live her new life to the full.

The night before the new academic year's commencement, Adolf offered Anna a dinner at one of the most renowned restaurants in town. That was a once-in-a-lifetime experience for her, and she believed that night would be the beginning of a dream.

"My love, I want to make you happy from now on, but I want you to know that I think this is a new life for me as well. I'll stand by you through thick and thin."

Raising his glass, he signalled to Anna to do the same.

"My sweet Anna, I swear I will always love and protect you for as long as I live. Thanks to you, I realised what life means. I will solve all your problems and never hide anything from you. Believe me when I say that my life has found a meaning today. So far, my life outside academia has been indifferent and dull. I'm sure this holds for you too. Today, I no longer see a young girl, but a mature woman. I swear I'll never make you sad or lonely.

I want to raise our family and give our children all the things we were deprived of. But, please, promise me that you'll always be by my side through thick and thin."

Standing still, holding a glass of red wine, with tears in her eyes, Anna touched his palm tenderly and could barely speak:

"Love, I want you to know that I still think I live in a dream and maybe I can't realise what's really going on. I also want to tell you that I've never loved a man most girls my age would love to have by their side. If what I feel right now are passion and love, then I'm the happiest woman in the world. I'll always be by your side, and I want to raise a beautiful family. I want it to grow fast, and I swear we will always live together to the bitter end."

That night ended as beautifully as it had started, to the magic sounds of Wagner.

Two years had passed since the day she saw Adolf, and only a few months since the moment her life changed. While attending to the house chores, Anna also did things outside of it. At first, by his side, accompanying him to almost every social gathering he was to attend—now they grew in number and interest. She began to take care of her physical appearance more than she used to. She wanted to shine next to him. It wasn't difficult for her as she was ravishing. Adolf, influenced by his studies on ancient Philosophy and Literature, often likened her to Goddess Venus.

A new maid had started working with them. She was a young girl from the province— an acquaintance of Adolf's aunt. He asked Anna to quit her studies, as they had agreed and promised to give her private tuition.So in the mornings while the professor was gone, Anna spent some time reading in the extensive library. She wanted to finish 'Medea,' the work of that ancient Greek tragedian. Its theme blew her mind when she heard that unknown professor analyse that wondrous heroine's deeds and character.

Of course, she did all this till the afternoon. Then, as soon as her beloved husband came back, she was completely devoted to him, but there was also Emma, her loyal friend. She didn't want to stop seeing her as she had known her for as long as she had known the professor. Mrs. Bird, her beloved mother, often visited her so that she wouldn't feel lonely, but Anna too paid her frequent visits, at Adolf's bidding. Deep down, she felt somewhat guilty for leaving her so soon. Therefore, this way, her life acquired some meaning, having all her loved ones by her side.

That winter seemed menacing. It was only October, yet grey Berlin was soon covered in snow.

Today, Anna was seeing Emma. She hadn't seen her for a long time, and in the afternoon, she was expecting to have lunch with her mother and Adolf. She would meet Emma at their favourite hang-out, at the cafe in the square. Whenever she saw her friend, she wanted to divest herself of the clothes of a mature woman and wife of a professor and become insouciant, just like she used to be. On the one hand, Emma was happy for her friend's bliss, but on the other, she was sad she had lost touch with her classmate.

"Good morning, my dear Emma! Let me look at you! You're splendid!"

"Good morning, girlie! Or should I say, Mrs. Krause?" Emma asked smilingly, hugging her best friend. "Come sit with me. I want you to tell me what your new life is like. I'm curious to know!"

"I'll tell you all about it, my dear. You can't imagine how much I needed to see you and have a chat!"

After ordering a hot coffee, Anna was quick to say laughingly:

"You tell me first. How are things in there? You know, in that vast amphitheatre...More specifically, in the second row, opposite the podium."

"Ah...you know, dear, another classmate with her friend occupied it. They also took my own seat as well. This year, I'm no longer sitting there. The first day I went to sit, it felt so cold—freezing cold, actually—, and next to me I could feel the absolute void," Emma answered bitterly, which didn't go unnoticed.

"I understand, my dear friend. You know, it all happened so fast that it hasn't sunk in yet. I thought that, despite the changes in my life, I would carry on with my studies. Still, Adolf—I want you to know that, apart from being an eminent scientist, he's also a serious and sensible man—asked me for some reasons I'm sure you're aware of to quit my studies and devote myself to the house chores and our family. He promised to offer me private tuition," Anna responded smilingly.

"You said you're going to raise a family, or am I mistaken? You mean you're expecting the heir?"

"Ah, no, no! We're just discussing this prospect. I mean, Adolf was the one to bring it up. I gather he wants to have a family—and he's in a hurry. You see, neither of us has any siblings, not to mention the fact that he's not that young..."

"How's Mrs. Bird? Is she sad that she has to live on her own? Tell me, why didn't you take her with you? As you said, your house is huge."

"I've asked her time and again, and so has Adolf, but she refused. She wants to stay with her memories, as she said. Of course, we visit each other very often. This afternoon, we'll be having lunch today."

Time flew. At some point, glimpsing at her watch, Anna rose from her seat, asked for the bill; after kissing her friend goodbye, she caught the bus back home. Just like she used to in the past, only now she wasn't going back to her paternal home, where she grew up and lived, but to her new place, the one her heart had chosen to spend for the rest of her life.

In the afternoon, Frieda, their new maid, a kindhearted polite girl, had prepared everything down to the minutest detail. Mrs. Bird and Adolf were waiting for her in the living room. She apologised for being late, hugged and kissed her mother, and then stole a kiss from her beloved Adolf before sitting between them. Seeing how beautiful their encounter was, Adolf felt the need to express his contentment.

"Mrs. Bird, once again, I would love to tell you that this place will always be open for you. I want you to feel at home in here, and let me suggest that you move in permanently. This way, you will be with your beloved daughter."

"Thank you once again, my child, but I've grown used to my abode. It's enough for me to see how happy my precious daughter is by your side. After all, we speak almost every day and visit each other quite frequently. All I want is to see you happy and hold my grandchild. I'm rather old, don't you forget that!" Mrs. Bird replied with a smile.

That day was so pleasant. Maybe for the first time in her life, Anna felt she was part of a complete family.

CHAPTER NINE

The predictions for a heavy winter were borne out day by day. Anna spent the best part of her time at home studying. For all the books he taught that year, Adolf made sure she could find them in their library. As Christmas drew closer, it was getting colder and colder. They had already put aunt Greta's invitation on the back-burner over and over again as she lived quite far. While the uni was closed due to bad weather, Adolf seized the opportunity to stay at home and keep company with Anna, which she found more than pleasant.

That morning, the snow, which kept falling, had covered everything outside. Anna had woken up very early, letting her beloved one get some rest. Today, she was going to have him all to herself. They would have some hot tea together and, if he felt like it, she would have him explain the modules he was teaching that year.

In a while, Adolf was downstairs. She happily prepared breakfast while he looked out the window. Seeing what the weather was like, he turned around and held her in his arms.

"Sweetheart, today and maybe the following days, we're going to be together all the time!"

"I'm so glad, my love! Fortunately, the weather is on my side, so you're given a chance to enjoy my company as a student as well, Professor!" Anna replied spontaneously.

"You're whining about that again," the professor remarked with a broad smile. "That's why you're going to sit here on the sofa and listen to me as I talk about another heroine in a different ancient Greek tragedy. I analysed her to my students last week."

"I'm all ears!" said Anna gleefully, and hastened to sit on the wide settee. He suddenly turned serious and started:

"Well, my dear, unique, and beautiful Miss Meisner, er…I'm sorry, I meant Mrs. Krause, today I'm going to tell you about another fateful wife found in another great ancient Greek work, 'Antigone.' She, together with her sister and two brothers, went through an indescribable family tragedy. They were all King Oedipus's children, who unwittingly married his own mother, so they were born out of this unholy marriage. When their father found out the truth, he left, haunted by his remorse, and gouged his own eyes out. As the two heirs to the throne were still young, Creon, their maternal uncle, became king. He was harsh, but loyal to the laws he laid down himself. When one of the two brothers grew up, he wanted to lay claim to the throne. In the big battle that ensued, they both got killed. Then, the king ordered to have only one buried while the other one, which militated against the regime, should remain unburied outside the town, at the mercy of wild animals."

Then, Antigone, his elder sister, reacted, which was inconceivable by society's standards back then, and tried to bury her brother on the sly. When she was arrested and asked by the king why she had gone against her own state laws, she courageously told him that sometimes moral law and the law of Gods were above humans' laws. That's what had driven her to that act.

"I stop here, dear Mrs. Krause, to remark that this heroine finally died. Besides, I think I've wearied you already, sweetheart."

"No, not at all! While listening to this remarkable story, I felt I was seated there in the second row, having before me the sweetest professor in the world. What an incredible story I've just heard! Full of turnovers…If I'm not mistaken, I think sometimes we obey what our soul, conscience, and morality dictate, ignoring even our own lives."

"Yes, that's what the tragedian wants to show: that sometimes in a person's life, although he or she knows the consequences, he's led to actions he believes to be right. With what he does, he thinks he purges his soul and conscience."

"What did you say the heroine's name was?"

"Antigone."

"Antigone and Medea. Two heroines are doing extreme things in their lives," Anna whispered. "To what extent does all this square with modern times and society?"

"These works, my love, are timeless. On the one hand, Medea's revenge and, on the other, the belief in the soul's morality as an act of purification of its remorse are two notions that existed and always will, as long as humans are alive."

"Well, the lesson is over, my beloved student. I've written quite a lot on all this and other equally important works. They're all in the library. You have the time to study them. If the weather improves over the following days, I'll call aunt Greta. She's invited us for lunch. She likes you a lot and wants to see you."

"Yes, we should go. I like her too. She's alone and our company will surely do her lots of good. After all, you are the only relative she's got—and the most beloved one!"

As Christmas drew closer, the weather got better and better. In a couple of days, the University would break up. Adolf had already called his aunt, and they would meet up the following week.

On Tuesday morning, after they came down their staircase, ready to meet aunt Greta, Anna was in for a big surprise. In front of their house was parked a grandiose black car, just like a real gentleman, Adolf opened the door for her to get in. It was the new car her loved one had bought.

"So that our dreams will travel for a while," he told her and tenderly kissed her on the cheek.

At a loss for words, Anna got in and, when he sat behind the wheel, she hugged and kissed him, whispering:

"'To the bitter end' is our vow. I'll never forget that, my love."

In a while, they stepped into his aunt's house. She was waiting for them at the entrance of her villa on the outskirts of the city. After her cordial welcome, they all sat in the drawing-room.

"At last, I see you after such a long time! I'm so happy!"

"We're just as happy, my dear aunt," said Anna. "We wanted to see you earlier, but the weather wasn't very nice."

"You're really ravishing and a wonderful person, sweetheart! I feel so happy that my beloved Adolf has known happiness by your side. You see, the war took away both his parents. Actually, he grew up alone and thanks to his inner strength, he accomplished all these things. He was only twenty-one when he lost his mother and father. He was still doing his military service, just like his father back then."

"Aunt, why are you raking over the ashes?" Adolf interrupted her somewhat irritatedly.

"It's OK. Let your aunt speak. I don't mind at all. Do you see? I've learnt something I didn't know—that you served in the army. You never mentioned that."

"My love, those were hard and bitter years, and I don't want to remember them. They're so at odds with my character, and I don't want to discuss them."

"I understand. My father, aunt Greta, served in the army too until late-1945, when he died of a heart attack. He worked as a diplomat at the Ministry of Foreign Affairs."

"Really, my girl?" exclaimed aunt Greta. "I didn't know that. Adolf's father was a high-ranking officer back then, and he probably knew him."

"Let's change the subject, shall we?" Adolf cut in, really pissed off this time.

"Alright, my boy. You're right. Besides, now that we've gathered together, I hope my sweet Anna will visit me more often, so we'll have plenty of time to discuss lots of things without any men treading on our toes," aunt Greta said with a loud laugh.

"That's for sure! I find your company so pleasant, my dear aunt!"

"I'm glad, my girl. You know, some very good friends often visit me for tea and a little bit of chat. Of course, you're much too young to put up with us, but you'll decide whether you can handle it."

"No, no, I'm eager to come. I enjoy your company, and I hope I'll enjoy spending time with your friends as well, but Adolf must agree to that."

"If you want that, honey, I have no objection," Adolf was quick to respond. While the women were talking, he was watching them with a sense of admiration, marvelling at the maturity with which Anna tackled the conversation.

In the afternoon, after lunch, they discussed the future of the newlyweds as well as various sociopolitical issues, mainly the economic boom of modern Western Germany. Of course, they didn't omit to refer to that ignominious Berlin Wall the other side erected, splitting a whole country in two.

CHAPTER TEN

New Year held in-store something pleasant for the young couple. Anna and Adolf visited the doctor at the hospital to make sure she was pregnant and discuss her course. Their happiness was complete. Adolf was on top of the world. Anna couldn't believe it. As soon as they got back home, Adolf, who was gripped by anxiety for the first time, asked her loved one to stay at home and not go out very often. He wanted to protect her till she gave birth at the end of the summer.

Straight away, Anna announced it to her mother, who couldn't wait to see her, so she visited her the very next morning. Her mother asked her if Anna wanted her to come over to take care of her, yet Anna wanted to do all this on her own. If she needed her mother's help, though, she would call her on the spot.

The first weeks ran smoothly, and Anna's pregnancy didn't have any complications. Mrs. Bird's visits were more and more frequent, so were Emma's. Anna's best friend was so happy for her. Even when he was away in the mornings, Adolf was always by her side, either physically or mentally, and the couple always visited the doctor together.

The beginning of summer found Anna in an advanced stage of pregnancy, and Adolf spent most of his time with her, especially after the end of the academic year. His main concern was how she would remain calm. Of course, just like many other couples, they wondered what the baby's sex might be. Adolf wanted it to be a boy, and Anna made no bones about wanting it to be a girl. Now that Adolf was constantly with her, Anna's mother didn't pay frequent visits; still, she called her every day. Even aunt Greta called her very often. For her, Adolf was her son, and she really cared about him and his wife.

This year's summer was quite cool, which made things easier for Anna as birth drew nearer. They visited their doctor much more often now, and everything was ready.

Late at night on September 3rd, labour pains commenced, and eight hours later, Anna brought a healthy child into the world. Everyone was outside her hospital ward that morning. Mrs. Bird, Emma, aunt Greta…From the moment they reached the hospital, Adolf didn't leave her side. He was so elated that he didn't stop hugging and kissing everyone.

Three days later, they went back home together with their new member, a beautiful daughter, who was the spitting image of her father. She had come at the right time to complete their bliss. A bliss they were both sure would last forever. Now Frieda had to attend to the house chores and Anna, especially during the first days, before she was ready to take over again. On the other hand, Anna already felt strong enough and happily announced to Adolf that she would take care of her daughter by herself, which made her beloved husband immensely happy.

This year flitted by for Adolf and Anna. Their child put the finishing touches on their bliss. After getting his fill of his daughter for almost a month, the professor went back to his academic duties. Justifiably, Anna now neglected Adolf as she spent most of her time taking care of their daughter. She wanted to show him love, even through Helga—that was the name they had agreed on over the first months of her pregnancy.

Whenever she had problems with the baby, she asked for Mrs. Bird's help. She wanted to take care of Helga with the same love and affection she had enjoyed as a child—from the moment she cried in her mother's arms. Now that she was a mother herself, she believed that this sacred bond forged inside the womb is so strong that nothing can break it. On the other hand, all these unprecedented things Anna felt couldn't in the least detract from her love for this man that came into her life to give her so much bliss. To the bitter end, as they vowed the moment they decided to be together forever.

The following months flew by. Anna's attention to Helga left no room for other things. She didn't leave the house very often, so her mother and her best friend Emma came to see her much more frequently—this time not only for Anna. Aunt Greta, though because of some health issues, couldn't pay them any visits. Besides, they didn't live very close. However, when Helga grew up a little, she asked her nephew to take her to her. She saw her just like a granddaughter. She wanted to see Anna again as she took to her. For her, she was the only woman who made so happy the man left in her life.

Emma was their most frequent visitor. She loved her friend so much that she was pleased with her happiness. Adolf, silent as always, took care of the two women of his life.

In mid-spring, Helga began to crawl and was in need of hugs and walks. Of course, her parents offered her whatever she wanted. Her mother spent many hours in the park every day, but now she wasn't all by herself. Her guardian angel was with her. On bank holidays, Adolf accompanied the two 'ladies', with a permanent smile across his lips, grateful for these two wonderful gifts. Two gifts that broke the monotony of his solitude as well as his long-standing sorrow and woes. Now, these two creatures came along to heal everything.

In a few days, the summer made its presence acutely felt. The University had closed down for a week now. This morning, Anna was in high spirits. Helga was sleeping in her room while she was waiting for Adolf to come down for breakfast.

"Good morning, love. Today, I see you're well-rested and more beautiful than ever!"

"Thank you, my charming professor, but you should know you must split your compliments in two from now on. If one of us gets jealous, woe betide you!" replied Anna laughingly and bent over to give him a tender kiss.

"Today, I have a proposal to make, which is a wedding gift and a present for the birth of our beloved daughter."

"What do you mean? Tell me! I'm all ears! Don't keep me in suspense!"

"Well, I think I'll offer you the trip I didn't manage to offer you last summer. That wonderful child sleeping in her crib came so unexpectedly!"

"Trip? What a wonderful gift! Let me guess!"

"Yes, the trip I went on a couple of years ago on my own, when my body was in Heaven, and my mind was here with you. Back then, I promised myself we would go on that trip together next time. What d'you think? I'm sure you've realised what I'm talking about! Do you accept my offer?"

"So darling, you mean that wonderful country where the sun is hotter than anywhere else in the world, Greece? Where summers are different, and all the beautiful plays you teach at the university are put on at the ancient theatres?"

"Exactly, sweetheart! It's the place where we'll stroll along the beautiful beaches together. You can't imagine what those islands, museums, and theatres are like. Some of the most renowned performances are put on there. To the best of my knowledge, your favourite 'Medea' is going to be performed this year."

"Oh, you make me so happy, darling!" Anna exclaimed in his arms. "But now we have a new member. Are we going to take Helga with us?"

"No, Helga is too young. This is going to be our honeymoon. Frieda will take care of our daughter while we're away. I know this will sadden you, just like me, but I really want to go on that trip with you. It's an opportunity for us to get some rest."

"Alright. I think we both need that. I'm going to call mother tomorrow to let her know. I'm sure she'll be happy about it. Ah, I forgot to tell you that, just as I came downstairs this morning, aunt Greta called. She's not feeling very well and, on top of that, she complained that we hadn't visited her. Actually, she asked me to have a cup of coffee with her tomorrow, if you're too tired. She'll invite a friend over. I gather she wants to see me more than you," Anna said smilingly.

"She's right, my dear. We've completely forgotten her and that's not very good. She loves you so much…Well, that's what we'll do. We'll see aunt Greta together, then Helga and I will leave later on. She'll see the baby as well. You'll stay there till afternoon; then I'll come to pick you up. Therefore, I'll have the chance to be with my daughter for a few hours. We'll get to know each other better," Adolf said. "You can inform your mother about our summer holidays the day after tomorrow."

The next morning, after they awakened Helga, they were ready to leave. In half an hour, the little princess stepped into aunt Greta's house for the first time. The old lady was so happy to hold her in her arms.

Adolf, who was in a hurry, apologised and stood up to hold Helga. However, he hadn't anticipated strict aunt Greta's reaction—just like a real mother and grandma; she demanded that little Helga stay with her in the house. Of course, Adolf had no option, but to buckle while Anna giggled at the spectacle.

For quite some time, until aunt Greta's friend came over, all eyes were on little Helga.

"As I told you, I've invited my favourite friend. We're having lunch together. You know, she's a regular visitor who keeps me company, especially now that I've become doddery. She's all alone in life."

"No problem, aunt. It's a pleasure to meet your friend, but maybe Helga will tire you."

"No, sweetheart! Her presence can only give us joy and a chance for Andrea to see my favourite granddaughter."

An hour later, the doorbell rang and a presentable lady turned up at the entrance. After they made the introductions within ten minutes, they were already having a warm and cordial conversation, as if they had known one another for years. Mrs. Andrea was a kind, beautiful, and loquacious woman.

"I'm so pleased to meet you, my dear girl. It's a pleasure to know that a beautiful young woman is at our beloved Adolf's side. Mrs. Greta thinks the world of you. That's the kind of person Adolf needed after so many hardships he went through from an early age. Now that I've made your acquaintance, I believe that you will make a perfect couple. Together with Helga, you're going to be a really happy family."

"Thank you so much for your kind words, Mrs. Andrea. I'm really touched, but what did you mean by Adolf's hardships? You obviously refer to the loss of his parents in the bombings."

"Er, yes…that's what I refer to. My dear, you can realise how hard it is to lose both your parents at such a tender age—only 21."

"I surely know what this feels like, Mrs. Andrea, since I too lost my father when I was only two."

Mrs. Greta abruptly interrupted their conversation.

"Come on, Andrea! Why should we talk about all these grim things now? So many years have passed. We needn't rake over the ashes."

"It's OK, my dear aunt. I don't bother. My mother too, avoids talking to me about the old times, but I want to hear and learn more about that hard period," said Anna.

"Alright, honey. I just want you not to worry as you're young. You and Adolf must look ahead. Therefore, carry on with your discussion, and I'll play with my granddaughter."

"Thank you so much for your love, aunt. So Mrs. Andrea, tell me about those years. As I said, my mother doesn't want to talk about that era. Actually, from an early age, she told me to look ahead. I can barely remember my father. I know him only from some photos and my mother's descriptions. I don't know if aunt Greta has told you, but my father was a high-ranking diplomatic officer at the Ministry of Foreign Affairs."

Upon hearing that, Mrs. Andrea suddenly interrupted her and, apologising, asked her:

"You said your father was a diplomat? What a coincidence, my dear!"

"I don't understand. What coincidence?" asked Anna in puzzlement.

"Well, let me make it clear. I'll tell you that I served in many posts at the Ministry of Foreign Affairs between 1938 and 1956, and I surely met your father. Let me guess. You said your father died when you were two."

"Yes, I was born in 1943..."

"Oh, God! I think I'm losing my mind now! Was your father's name Hans?"

"Yes. Hans Meisner. Did you know him?" asked Anna.

Mrs. Andrea leapt to her feet, as if electrocuted, stood still, spread her arms open, and held Anna's hands. She stared at her for a few seconds, then told her when she got over the shock:

"So before me stands Hans and Bird Meisner's daughter? That littledoll he brought to the Ministry when she was two months, and showed her to us as the greatest gift life had given him, as he said? It seems like only yesterday! There's so much more, my love!"

"What a coincidence!" remarked Anna touched. "So you also know my mother?"

"Of course! I suppose she remembers me too. She often came to the Ministry when your father served in Berlin. She followed him wherever he went abroad, at the embassies and consulates."

"Tell me, how was my father at work?"

"You know, my dear Anna, I wasn't a high-ranking officer in there. I slowly rose through the ranks. It took me five years. Still, I really liked and appreciated your father. Don't you think there was something between us! He was a very serious man dedicated to his job. What I distinctly remember is how happy he was when he announced the birth of his daughter. As you may already know, there was a small age difference between him and your mother, and he often expressed his desire to have a baby. However, my dear Anna, I must apologise to you again for telling you all this, but, you know, as your aunt keeps saying, I talk too much! I'm sorry."

But Anna needed to know, as she travelled back in time. She wanted to find out things her mother had never told her about or avoided discussing. She saw that woman in front of her like a closed book that she had to open up and start reading.

"Please, go ahead, Mrs. Andrea. Please! Since you say my parents felt the need to have a baby, do you remember the day I was born?"

"Why do you ask me this, my girl? Parents say all these pleasant things to their children."

"Sorry to insist but, as I told you before, I don't remember anything about these two years of my life, until my father died. You see, it was the war and, as my father passed away so suddenly, my mother had told me very little."

That very moment, as if snapping out of a dream that made her speak all the time without realising what she said, Andrea shot to her feet and said agitatedly:

"My dear Anna, my beautiful girl, I think I upset you with my words. This day has been quite a surprise to me after our acquaintance. I want to tell you that you can't imagine how happy I am to have met you. I also want to put an end to our discussion, if you don't mind. Let's spend some time with our hostess and your pretty daughter. All I can tell you today is that you should know life sometimes hides certain things from us and defines our course against our will."

"What are you talking about, Mrs. Andrea? Why are you telling me all this? Are you hiding something? The fact that you put an end to his discussion so abruptly makes me wonder."

"You're right, my child. I've just met you, but I want you to trust me and consider me a very good friend. I know I've made you wonder, but please let's not carry on with this conversation in your aunt's place. Let me ask for a favour: Don't tell your mother or Adolf about meeting me. I promise to get together and talk soon. I'll tell you more. Do you promise?"

"I promise because I feel a weird void inside of me. Give me your phone number so that I can call you."

That very moment, Helga's cry upstairs brought Anna back to reality with a bump. It was time to prepare her food, then sample aunt Greta's cuisine. Anna didn't really feel like eating anything after that conversation. Apart from her questions that had gone unanswered, there was an indeterminate sense of fear in her soul.

During the meal, Anna tried not to let her agitation show on her face—she didn't want aunt Greta to see that something was going on. Over the next three hours, Anna was much calmer, and the three ladies were already talking about the country's political, economic, and cultural situation. After all, aunt Greta's friend, Andrea, seemed to be quite knowledgeable about the arts and culture in general, which endeared her to Anna. Mrs. Andrea mentioned Adolf's significant contribution to the academic community as he held a very important post.

"My dear Anna, I've learnt that this love affair began in the amphitheatre, is that right?"

"Yes, yes," Anna replied somewhat tentatively. "I couldn't resist his looks and personality," she added laughingly.

"Adolf, my favourite nephew, is an eminent scholar and a very kind man," added aunt smilingly.

"That's right. Actually, as far as I know, he adores Classical Studies and Philosophy, especially ancient Greek philosophy. Am I wrong?" asked Mrs. Andrea.

"Yes, that's true. I've been bitten by the same 'bug,' actually! I've already studied two great works under his supervision and, now that I've quit my studies as I want to raise my child, he offers me private tuition! Ah! Auntie, I forgot to tell you: in a few days, Adolf is going to give me my wedding gift: a trip to a very beautiful country, as he told me— Greece. It's a country with the most beautiful islands in the world. Of course, we're mainly going to visit museums and ancient theatres, where the astounding works of antiquity poets are still put on. That's the works Adolf teaches."

"Splendid! I'm so glad!" replied Aunt Greta. "You know, after he lost his parents, Adolf wanted to leave all his previous life behind and decided to devote himself to studying and teaching. Through these works, he loved this beautiful country you're going to on holiday."

"What do you say of all this, Mrs. Andrea?" Anna asked her somewhat abruptly, seeing her inscrutable face.

"Yes, yes...I've heard about Greece too. I don't know. I hope you'll like it..."

This answer didn't sit comfortably with Anna. The eyes of the middle-aged woman she had met a few hours earlier struck terror in her heart, and this feeling, instead of putting her off, actually drew her closer to her.

"I'll tell you all about it when we come back," Anna said to both women, just as the doorbell rang. Anna hadn't realised how fast time flew. Today, she felt something strange had happened deep within. Adolf didn't stay at all. After kindly greeting Mrs. Andrea, he hugged his beloved daughter, kissed his aunt, and they all made for the car.

Anna whispered in Mrs. Andrea's ear that they would soon get together after returning from the holidays.

"It was great meeting you, my dear Anna. See you soon. Adolf, from the bottom of my heart, I hope you'll have a great time in Greece and wish you the best of luck."

A few days later, Anna and Adolf were flying over the clouds on board the plane bound for that southern European country, Greece, where they were planning to spend their summer holiday. During the flight, Anna looked in high spirits, but deep down, she felt scared from the moment she met aunt Greta's strange friend. Although he suspected that something was going on, Adolf didn't take much heed as he thought it was their daughter's absence that made his wife feel dejected. But now, he had to do all he could to make his adorable wife feel on top of the world so that they could have a great time during the summer. As this was Anna's first flight, he held her hand until touchdown.

"Sweetheart, I see something's troubling you. If you're thinking of Helga, let me tell you that you needn't worry. Rest assured that your mother and Frieda will put out all the stops to make our daughter feel great. It's the first summer we're spending together. I want this to be a good start for the rest of our lives. We're going to rent a spacious car with a chauffeur, and visit almost all the museums and ancient theatres this country boasts. Then, we'll find a well-known destination to enjoy the sun and the sea."

Adolf's words took Anna's mind off things. She really needed to change her mood and rejoice. As soon as the plane landed, they both felt the heat and the sun on their faces.

"The weather's so different from Berlin…," Anna states. "People here must be really happy!"

"Things are not quite like that," said Adolf inside the taxi that drove them to the hotel. "This country was at war with ours and, just like all other countries, it too paid a heavy price in terms of disasters and human lives. Everyone paid in this destructive war and, as you've seen for yourself, our country too paid and is still paying the price, but let's not dwell on this right now…We came here because, if you remember, last time I was here on my own, as a guest, I had promised myself that we'd be together next time. I was so sure that we were going to spend the rest of our lives together! To the bitter end, my love! Like we swore to each other."

"You're right, darling. I promise I'll leave it all behind and be with you all the time, body and soul so that we'll spend the best holiday ever!" said Anna and kissed him tenderly, as they walked into the hotel.

After they rested the first day, a luxury car with a chauffeur awaited them at the entrance the next morning. He would show them around the city's attractions. It was a city full of history and civilisation. In a while, Adolf and Anna were walking hand-in-hand along the streets and alleys of one of the most renowned monuments in the world, the Parthenon, which had stood haughtily on top of the sacred rock of the Acropolis for over 2.500 years. Adolf kept talking to her about the history of this holy monument. Then, they visited the famous ancient Odeon of Herodes Atticus, where the greatest plays and concerts were put on to date. As if he were in his university amphitheatre, Adolf couldn't stop telling her about those poets and authors of Antiquity who lived and excelled in that very place. Bewitched, Anna was gaping at all those miraculous things around her.

"So my love, you mean that these two famous plays, 'Antigone' and 'Medea,' mainly the latter, impresses me the more without knowing the reason why they were played and still are in this very theatre?"

"Precisely! But I have a big surprise for you tomorrow! We're going to visit another more famous theatre, in another town, Epidaurus. This theatre is famous for its acoustics, and plays are performed without any devices."

The next day, the driver took them to Epidaurus through a difficult course. A cobbled uphill road led them to the open stone theatre, which was so majestic in terms of architecture and position. There were lots of people—after all, hundreds of them visited this sacred place on an everyday basis.

"Sweetheart, here the architect, who built this theatre thousands of years ago, made its acoustics so perfect that the audience can clearly hear the actors' words even from the highest seats. This is where all these wonderful plays I am honoured to teach at the uni are being played to date. 'Antigone,' 'Medea,' which is your favourite, and many more I will teach you in our home-based amphitheatre this year are played almost every year," Adolf told her laughingly. "We have so many years ahead of us to visit these places again and again—not only these; there are many more interesting locations." Anna felt on top of the world, seeing all this.

"I don't know why, my love, but I've been in high spirits since we set foot in this wonderful country. I could easily live here."

"All this is so beautiful, but so are the coming days. Tomorrow, we're going to sail to a big—the biggest, actually!—island, where most visitors are German. Acquaintances and friends who have been there have told me they'd had a fantastic time there!"

The following days were incredible for the young couple. They went for a swim at majestic beaches, ate delicious food at traditional small taverns, and visited archaeological sites. Anna didn't want to go back. Helga was surely looking for her as it was the first time she had parted with her. Of course, she spoke to her mother every day, and she was happy that grandma and granddaughter got on so well.

On the other hand, though, there was a loose end she had to tie up—it had completely slipped her mind all these days. A loose end that came into her life out of the blue and began to pester her. She was consumed with thought the moment she boarded the plane for Germany.

This morning was different for Anna. As the summer drew to a close, the weather in Berlin got chillier again. Today, Anna found it hard to wake up, as if sleep wanted to pin her to her bed. She slowly and weariedly went down to the kitchen to prepare breakfast before

Adolf joined her. She had been preparing breakfast on her own ever since she got married. Today, though, her gaze and moves showed that something was troubling her without even realizing it, which didn't go unnoticed.

"What's the matter, love? You look somewhat pale like something's pestering you. Is something the matter?"

"Nothing special. I'm just feeling a little tired, that's all."

After breakfast, she went upstairs to Helga's room. She did that every single day. Today, though, as she saw her sleeping, she stood still beside her and a teardrop trickled down her cheek. That was the first time she had ever done that—without rhyme or reason. She tried to smile, but suddenly a sense of fear gripped her; she leapt to her feet and took a step back.

"What's happening to me?" she wondered and stepped out of the room without kissing her baby.

Upset as she was, but unable to check it, she ran down the stairs to throw herself into Adolf's arms.

"What's going on, sweetheart?" he asked her. But, without speaking, she clutched him like a scared bird, as if she didn't want to let him go to the university. He stroked her hair tenderly, reassured her, and asked her again:

"My sweet Anna, what's the matter? Please tell me. I'm the only person you have in life, right? The only one you can trust?"

"I don't know; I can't understand what's happening to me today. I didn't sleep very well last night. I kept having nightmares."

Adolf kissed her with affection, had her sit on the couch in the living room, and promised not to go to the uni today to spend the whole day with her.

"No, no, I'll be fine! You must go to work! I'm thinking of calling Emma to go out for a coffee. I hope to feel better. I guess it's because I didn't sleep."

"Alright. I agree. You should go out with Emma if that's going to do you good. If not, call me to come over."

After a while, Anna called Emma and went upstairs to Helga's room. She couldn't leave without kissing her daughter. An hour later, she was sipping a hot cup of coffee with her favourite friend, who always did what Anna liked. Still, she couldn't hide her tension and agitation from Emma either.

"What's wrong with you? And make sure you don't lie to me because I'm sure something's going on!"

"I don't know, girl. I plunged into a deep slumber last night and kept having nightmares. I guess that's what's happening. I'll be fine. What's up?"

"No news is good news!" Emma replied smilingly. "Tell me in great detail how your holiday was. I didn't understand much over the phone."

"Oh, it was the most beautiful trip of my life! What am I saying? It was the only trip I've ever been on! I saw such unique places in a beautiful hot country! Above all, you know, I saw those ancient magic theatres at close quarters, where the plays Adolf teaches are still performed! Our professor actually promised to take me to Greece again next summer if my favourite 'Medea' is put on at the Theatre of Epidaurus."

Anna seemed to feel much more relaxed after this chat, but still, something was bugging her. After she came back from Greece, she didn't call Mrs. Andrea straight away. For her, she was a strange lady that had thrown a spanner in the works with her words. Maybe what lay behind her reluctance to contact her was the suspicion that there had been something more than a mere friendship between Mrs. Andrea and Anna's father. Emma, who always read her soul, asked her again:

"When you relax, I want you to tell me about it, please. I want you to know that I'm here for you and always will. I consider you my best friend. I'll always be there for you."

"Thanks once again, my dear Emma. I hadn't told you anything about an event that happened before we left for our summer holiday. Maybe that's what's behind my mood. I tried to forget it as it caused me an indeterminate sense of fear, but it constantly flashes through my mind!"

"What is it, Anna? It must be something really serious, as far as I can see..."

"No, I don't know anything yet, but that's what happened. Before we left for holiday, we all visited aunt Greta. Adolf didn't stay. He actually left Helga behind and he came to pick her up late in the afternoon. That day, a friend of aunt Greta's came along, Mrs. Andrea. At some point, we were left alone since aunt Greta took Helga upstairs to play with her. This lady worked at the Ministry of Foreign Affairs for years. That's where my father used to work. She knew him very well and held him in high regard. The strange thing is, she even remembered me. Actually, she stressed the fact that my father was on top of the world when I was born because, as she told me, my parents took a long time to have a baby. Note that I never heard my mother say such a thing. Mrs. Andrea told me many other things—she was really talkative, you know, but all this made me wonder. As we talked, her words got weirder and weirder, as if she knew parts of my life that I wasn't even aware of. Her eyes showed me that she's hiding some secrets, which caused me an indeterminate sense of fear."

"When I insisted that she explain to me, she suddenly shot to her feet and said hurriedly that we would meet up again; she would tell me more. Actually, she gave me her phone number, so that I would call her. Her words showed a kind of determination that really scared me and piqued my curiosity at the same time. I don't know what to do, girl. On the one hand, I want to know, but I feel scared and threatened. The strange thing is, she asked me not to say anything about our meeting—not even to Adolf! What am I supposed to do?"

"You must see her; otherwise, all this will keep torturing you, affecting your life. The fact that she asked you not to say anything to the others shows how serious the situation is. I'm nothing loath to help you. Has it occurred to you that this woman could have had a special or clandestine affair with your father—even if it was only platonic or unrequited?"

"Yes, it has, and I find it scary! Still, even if it's true, why would she ever reveal it to me? There's no reason why she should do it now. Anyway, thanks once again, honey. You're the only person I can trust. I'll call her and let you know. Tell me, how's School this year?"

"Well, I'm all, but finished. I need to sit one exam, and I'm done! Our professor, you know, has a soft spot for me, and I think he's more lenient," Emma replied laughingly.

The next day, after Adolf left for the uni, Anna went to her home library to read her favourite book, 'Medea.' In its pages, she had hidden Mrs. Andrea's phone number.

"Hello? Who is it?"

"Good morning, Mrs. Andrea. It's me, Anna, Adolf's wife. How are you?"

"Good morning, my dear Anna! I'm so glad to hear you! After that meeting at your aunt's place, I was afraid you might not call me. It's true that I made you wonder, but I want you to know I was so surprised to make your acquaintance that I was completely carried away, especially when I learnt who you are. I said things I shouldn't have said. Tell me, are you alright?"

"Mrs. Andrea, it's a fact that hearing you tell me all these things scared the wits out of me. When your face suddenly changed and you stopped talking, I had so many questions that I couldn't find peace. Then, Adolf and I left for Greece, a country with so much beauty and history, and our trip took my mind off things. And I can say I fell in love with this place the moment I set foot there," said Anna.

"I'll tell you a big truth, my dear. I've thought all this over. Sometimes, truth in life may do us more harm than good."

"What do you mean? Are there things concerning me that I don't know? Do you mean to tell me that there's a big truth hiding somewhere? Please, don't keep me in suspense. Tell me when and where we're going to meet."

"Alright, honey. Bear in mind, though that you're going to hear things that will affect you for the rest of your life. If you ask me why I want to talk to you, I'll open my heart and tell you some truths, not only about your life, but also mine, as they have so much in common. If you're ready, we can meet at my place today, but promise me this will stay between us. To shake off that fear you feel, I want you to trust me in your father's memory. I liked him a lot!"

"Alright, my instinct tells me to trust you. Give me your address, and I'll be there in a couple of hours. Whatever we say will stay between us—I promise."

In two hours, the door of a small apartment in an impoverished area of the town opened up and Anna walked into a room that was to change her life forever.

"Welcome, my sweet girl," said Mrs. Andrea, as he tenderly held her hand and kissed her. "Tea or coffee?"

"Hi, Mrs. Andrea. I'd prefer coffee. As I don't have much time on my hands, and this is the first time I've hidden from my mother and husband, let's cut to the chase, right?"

"Alright, Anna, I understand. Before I talk about you, though, please bear with me for a while. I'll tell you my own story first. It's a story that began 26 years ago. I'll reveal my own deep secrets as I'm sure you'll better understand your own truths.

"The moment I met you and realised who you really are, I decided that you will be the only person in my life I will share my story and truth with. Maybe what you're going to hear will sound indifferent, but don't interrupt me."

"I promise to hear attentively," replied Anna, who was calm.

"My dear Anna, as you've probably realised, I'm an old and long-suffering woman. I don't care about my life anymore. Please don't interrupt me so that I'll be able to put everything in order and not forget anything."

Two years before that horrible World War broke out, I lived in a rich and beautiful Berlin suburb with my parents and three siblings. That year, 1937, the German regime clamped down on the rich Jewish families. People were killed and entire families were wiped off the face of the earth, unable to react. Back then, I was having an affair with a young university student—he was handsome, tall, and sturdy, but my father wouldn't approve of him. One day, which was a tragic fateful day for my family, on my way back home, I heard the neighbours say that the police had arrested my whole family—my parents and my three younger siblings. I was simply the lucky one as I was at the uni at the time. I ran away, beside myself, and tried to find them—with the help of my boyfriend and other connections I had. Unfortunately, I found out that they had been taken to a camp. A neighbour told me that they were also looking for me, so I hid away and escaped death.

"To cut a long story short, I never found my family, and my friend, who truly loved me, just before he did his military service, managed to get me a fake ID—as he had some connections with the regime—and some money. Since then, I've been called Andrea Emberhand. Thanks to him, I'm still alive! But this wasn't the only good thing that wonderful man did for me. He had me hired as a cleaning lady by the Ministry of Foreign Affairs as I didn't have a single penny to my name after my parents' death. I rose through the ranks during the war, and then I became a clerk as I was educated enough. It's there that I met an exceptional high-ranking diplomat, Mr. Hans Meisner, your father."

"This means you're Jewish, Mrs. Andrea?" Anna asked, shaken by what she had heard. "So you used to have a different name."

"That's right. My real name is Sarah, and this is the secret I will take to my grave."

"Why didn't you change your name again after the war? What about your friend?"

"Ah, that was another tragedy! My friend, my dear Krug, saved my life, but lost his own during the war. You see, fate has other designs. I had no reason or strength to make changes in my life. I kept working there as I had to earn a living."

Touched by what she was hearing, Anna stood up and hugged that lady standing before her. After a few minutes, inside her warm embrace, she plucked up the courage to say something about the woman's tragedy.

"My dear Andrea or Sarah, I honestly have to confess that while you were talking, I felt shocked and I'm really sorry about what happened. I must also thank you for sharing all your secrets with me, although we barely know each other. Still, you have to tell me how all this relates to me. You said earlier that fate and human luck sometimes look alike, and now I'm getting scared."

After taking a sip of her coffee, Mrs. Andrea or Sarah asked Anna if she was ready to hear all the things that concerned her.

"I'm ready, Mrs. Sarah. I'm all ears."

"Before I begin to talk about you, my sweet girl, I have to tell you something else first. As soon as I found out who you are, I decided to talk to you and reveal my true identity as, many years ago, at the age of 21, if I'm not mistaken, a gentleman much older than me fancied me, but this didn't go any further. This man was the only one who replaced the person who saved my life. He was a real friend; we talked about everything—nothing more than that. Of course, I was too scared to share my secret with him, but he wouldn't hide anything from me. He often talked to me about his problems. He had been married to your mother for many years. He loved her, but they both wanted to have a child. Shall I carry on, my dear, or are you getting tired?"

Anna simply nodded her head.

"This remarkable man developed into a high-ranking diplomat then was transferred abroad as ambassador and consul. It goes without saying that he served the regime, which held sway in Germany during the war as well."

"You're obviously talking about my father now," Anna interrupted her, as she was overcome with the same fear.

"Yes, my dear Anna. Let me explain why I'm revealing my true identity today. I made this decision because, at the end of the war, a few months before he passed away, your father shared his greatest secret with me. Are you ready to hear it, or shall we stop our conversation here and never refer to it again?"

Feeling a bad hunch, Anna stood up and moved to the other side of the room.

"Wait a minute, Mrs. Andrea. Please give me some time to take a breath. Then, we can surely carry on."

Being tense too, Sarah asked her again if they should put an end to their discussion.

"No, no, please, wait for a second. I'm ready and determined to hear what you have to say, no matter how hard," Anna replied.

After a few minutes, Anna took her seat, not opposite Sarah, but right beside her. She held her hand and asked her to continue after she posed a serious question:

"Mrs. Sarah, I want you to tell me if you ever had an affair with my father."

"No, no, don't even think about it! I told you earlier: I was friends with your father, and our friendship was real and strong. I looked upon him as my protector after all I'd been through in my life."

"What I'm going to reveal to you, if you're ready, has to do only with you, and I want you to know that your father had me swear that I would never tell anyone. What I'm doing is a breach of promise, although I know that God wouldn't like such great truths—no matter how harsh—to be kept secret."

After giving Anna a tight hug, she continued talking in a whisper, as if she were afraid that someone might hear her.

"As I said, your father was really sad, just like your mother, as they couldn't have a baby. In the middle of the war, your father, Hans Meisner, served as consul in that beautiful country you went to on holiday. Greece as well as entire Europe was under German occupation. His position, though, wasn't in Athens, but the second biggest city, Salonica, a beautiful coastal place with a long history."

Anna, still and cold, threw herself into Mrs. Sarah's arms.

"In this beautiful big city, Salonica lived a great number of wealthy Jewish Greek families, who ruled the whole country's trade. Like I told you earlier, every country occupied by Germany went through Hitler's manhunt and homicides. In March 1943, one of the S-S officials commanded that 15000 Jews living in this town were arrested and then taken to a horrible concentration camp called Auschwitz. There, innumerable Jews were killed in gas chambers within only a few days. Shall I continue, my dear?"

Anna felt numb all over her body. She couldn't utter a word. All she could do was signal to her to go ahead.

"Among these Jewish families was a young couple, a rich merchant and his wife. This woman was very pretty, as your father told me. Your parents knew them as they were their neighbours. They lived downtown in a mansion by the sea. The day they were arrested, a terrible mistake was made during the house search. A two-month-old angel was sleeping upstairs—it must have been fast asleep as no one realised it was there. Maybe the girl's mother did all she could to save her. The neighbour, the lady who lived next door—her name was Bird Meisner—, happened to be passing by the house a while after the incident and heard the baby's cries. As she saw nobody in the house, she knocked on the door and, getting no reply, pushed the door open and walked in. The baby's cries led her upstairs, where she saw a beautiful girl in her crib. She shouted, looked around, got outside, and found out what had happened. Without much thought, she took that baby angel home. You want to know what happened next, my dear?"

Anna slowly raised her eyes that were puffy, although she hadn't shed a tear. She couldn't say anything. She stood there transfixed. Mrs. Andrea was still holding her tight, fearing that something bad might happen to her. Anna realised it, held the old lady's hands, and faltered:

"No, don't worry. I'm fine. I just felt a void inside of me. Can I have a second coffee? That will help me a lot. Then, we can continue."

"I only want you to know, honey, that I don't mean to harm you. It's just that, when I found out who you are, I saw my own life in yours…"

Anna was too weak to cry, which would surely lift this burden off her chest. After a while, when she felt much better, she looked Mrs. Sarah in the eye and asked to continue the narration herself.

"This little baby, Mrs. Sarah, whose name nobody knew, changed identity and met her new parents, those who saved her life, loved her and brought her up like their own child. From what I've gathered, when my parents came back to their country, they presented me as their biological child."

"Of course, my mother, Mrs. Bird, was supposed to have given birth in the city where her husband served as consul."

"Exactly, my dear Anna. I want you to know that your parents, Hans and Mrs. Bird, loved you like real parents, and if you're alive today, this is thanks to Mrs. Bird's heart because she acted like a real mother. I understand that, after all this, you feel empty inside. I may have caused a terribly huge problem to your mother, but I made this decision in the memory of your biological parents, whom you didn't have the chance to meet. For the sake of their horrible and unfair death, I was so confused all this time. I didn't know if I should reveal it to you or not. Maybe Hans didn't want to take it to his grave when he confessed it to me."

Snapping out of her shock, Anna replied:

"No, no. It was wise of you to talk to me. My mother should have told me, as I grew up. She's responsible for that. Didn't she have to talk to me about my biological parents, the way they died, her own country's responsibility for their cruel deaths?" Now she burst into tears.

Sarah held her in her arms and let her get it all off her chest. She was very young, and this situation was too hard for her to cope with.

Anna felt better in a while, her bloodshot eyes showing her pain.

"What am I supposed to do now? How will I carry on with my life? How will I look my mother in the eyes? What will I say to Adolf? How will I raise my own daughter with all this pain in my heart?"

"My sweet Anna, humans have so much courage and strength. They can carry on with their lives in the teeth of adversity. Like I carried on with my own life when I lost everything. I'll be by your side to help you get over it. I changed my identity to continue living. You had your own identity changed so that you would start your life from scratch. Don't blame Mrs. Bird. In that horrible war, she felt like a real mother, and I believe that's how she raised you. I know how difficult it is for you to cope with this situation. I'll always be by your side. Fate often writes the story of our life without asking for our permission. Helga's presence will give you more strength than what you think you have."

"As for your mother, I think you must talk to her at some point. You shouldn't tell her about me as you may have to reveal my own secret as well. If you make up your mind, though, I believe your mother won't deny it. But, please, don't tell Adolf. Don't ruin your family's peace and quiet. Adolf is German, and I don't know how he's going to take it since he's been brought up by a military family that served the Nazi regime in many posts during the war, as his aunt told me."

"I'll think about talking to my mother, but why are you telling me this about Adolf? There's a gap here as well, or am I wrong?"

"No, honey. What are you thinking about?" Sarah instantly said. "Well, I'm afraid of what will come next. I simply mean that it's better to leave Adolf out of this."

"Yes, but you leave me with so many questions unanswered. You know how much I love and trust Adolf, and I believe that if I tell him about all this, he will stand by me as much as he can. I don't want to keep secrets from him."

"What I mean is that you must first sort this out with your mother before you tell Adolf, but not now. Please, trust me."

"Mrs. Andrea, we've been talking about Hans and Mrs. Bird all this time. You haven't told me anything about my real parents, about the mother who gave birth to me and why all those horrible things were done. Is it certain that they were murdered in those—what did you call them?—gas chambers? Is there a possibility that they might still be alive, looking for me, but unable to find me since Mrs. Bird made sure to change my identity? That's why I said I'd talk to Adolf, in case he and his connections could help me find some clues in that town in Poland, where that camp is."

"No, no, this must not be done. Don't rake over the ashes. This can only worsen things. First of all, darling, you must sort this out with your mother. Your birth info must have changed the moment you came here with Mrs. Bird and Hans as your biological parents. Once again, I plead with you not to involve Adolf in this story—for the time being. Don't forget that his father served the previous regime in high-ranking posts, and he may not want to be part of all this. To the best of my memory, Mrs. Greta has told me that he always wanted to forget this bleak past; that's why he studied Philosophy. Like I said earlier, you have to keep your own family away from your personal problem. This will help you carry on with your life."

"I don't know, Mrs. Sarah. I'll see what I can do. You turned my whole life upside down today. Why did you do that? Why do I have to believe you? You suddenly came into my life, and this will change once and for all. When these terrible things happened to your own family, you were old and mature enough to live all those truths as you told me. How can I readily believe all this? If all this is true, how will I move on? How will I look at my mother again? How will she react when I talk to her? What if she tells me all this is a pack of lies? You see what I've got myself into?"

Seeing how Anna reacted, Sarah felt scared, threw her arms around her again, and led her to the big sofa.

"My sweet Anna, please calm down. You're right. That's why I asked to see you on the phone. All this is true. I know sometimes the truth is harsh but, believe me, I fought hard before I decided to talk to you. Everyone must know the truth. We ourselves must rule our fate, no one else. If I'm wrong, I must apologise. It's easy for you to think all this is a lie. If that's what you think, we'd better leave everything as is. First of all, calm down, then we'll think about what's best for your life. When the man the war took away from me wanted to save my life by changing my identity, I got shocked at first before I decided to do it. I know some decisions are so hard to make. No matter how hard, what I told you is the truth. I want you to calm down, think rationally, and then make up your mind. I'll be there for you."

Despite her phobias, Anna seemed to have taken to this woman. After a while, she was much calmer and turned to Mrs. Sarah, saying:

"No hard feelings. Deep down, I'm convinced that what you told me is a tragic truth. It's just that I'm scared and don't know how to cope with it. What I'll never manage to find out without Adolf's help is what happened to my biological parents."

After a few minutes, Anna stood up and, looking at the clock on the wall, realised she was late. Within three hours, a whole page in her book of life had changed. After she cordially said goodbye, she said:

"Today, my dear Sarah, my life has turned upside down and I suppose it will be stigmatised forever. On the one hand, I'm grateful to you as I believe you talked to me sincerely. On the other hand, though, maybe if I hadn't learnt about all this, my life would be better, with me living in the middle of all these lies. I don't know. Everything's so slurred inside of me."

"My sweet Anna, life's often full of big or small reversals. What happened to you today is a big one. Tomorrow, it may look small compared to a bigger reversal."

Anna stopped short.

"What are you suggesting now? I think you're dropping hints again."

"It's nothing, sweetheart. It's just that, after what I've been through in my life, I've learnt to deal with difficult situations. If you trust me even a little, I'd tell you once more not to involve your own family—I mean Adolf and Helga—in this personal matter. If you muster up the courage, you can learn everything from your mother. After all, don't forget that this woman didn't give birth to you, but she gave you the chance to live on."

Upon hearing his, Anna hugged Sarah and burst into tears. She thanked her once again and said:

"If all this is true, which I feel it is, from this point onwards, I consider you my best friend, together with Emma."

CHAPTER ELEVEN

It was getting dark and Anna kept walking along the street fearlessly, not giving a damn about whether she was late and the others were worried. All that strange mood she had been in over the previous days foreboded this day. She would love to wake up and discover that all this was just a dream—a nightmare. Why had that woman chosen her? What about her acquaintance with Anna's father? Why had she shared such a great secret with her? Was something going on between them?

Her fatigue and weakness led her to the nearest taxi rank. She didn't care about the others' reactions. Her mind was stuck there, in that lonely woman's small flat, where hours earlier an episode of her own tragedy had been written.

After using Emma as an excuse to reassure Adolf, she went straight to her room, on the pretext of feeling tired. Adolf, who was waiting for her with bated breath, showed some understanding and didn't disturb her until he went to bed.

The next day, Anna had a lie-in. When she went downstairs, Adolf was already gone for the Uni, having asked Frieda to let him know if Anna didn't feel well.

"Shall I make tea or coffee, madam?"

"No, thank you, Frieda. I'm not in the mood. Maybe later. Today, I want you to spend some time with Helga. I want to be left alone in the office. I have some things to do," replied Anna.

She didn't want to be disturbed until her husband came back in the afternoon. She wanted to think about what she was going to do with her mother and how she could hide such a big secret. Today, she seemed to have got over the shock to some degree. She had to face the problem with a cool head. This strange woman, Sarah, must have given her strength to find out the truth. Anna felt this was a new day, completely different from all the others as if her soul were stronger now. She felt she was a different person. She sat at the desk in front of the bookcase and plunged into thought.

"Maybe all this is a big lie, a nightmare. Maybe Mrs. Andrea is simply a lunatic! No, she hasn't shown such signs. She was sure of what she said. Why did she reveal her own secret to me after so many years? She told me our lives have so much in common. The fact that she worked with my father in the same agency makes it all so convincing. There seems to have been a kind of erotic relationship between them; otherwise, he wouldn't have entrusted her with such a big secret. As she said, the Nazi killed her parents; then they conquered the country I was born in. Both families were Jewish citizens. Mrs. Sarah was saved by her young lover, a German who got killed when the war broke out after he had her change her name and identity. A German lady, Mrs. Bird, saved me, and I owe it to her and Hans, but she should have told me the truth when I grew up, shouldn't she? I love my mother so much! That's the one I knew as my real mother. What about my real parents, though? Why did all this happen? Why did they deprive me of their presence? Why were they taken away from me? Why didn't they let them bring me up? What was that war, after all? It wreaked such havoc with humanity! What's my own country? The one I was born in or the one I live in? We learnt at school that your country is the one you come from—the one you were born in. The place is stated in my documents. Where are my own documents? They changed my identity in order to carry on with my life. Just like in Sarah's case. What am I supposed to do now? Why would this ever happen to me? What about my mother, Mrs. Bird? She gave me a good upbringing; she paid for my education, she's so happy about my progress and marriage to an incredible man, although she raised some objections at first. Why did she? What hides behind that? No! If I remember well, she said I was still too young to get married. Still, when I tried to hide my relationship with him, she told me strictly that we shouldn't have secrets. And, when she assured me that she had never held a secret from me, I was convinced to talk to her. Yet, she concealed the biggest truth of my life. Wasn't she afraid that all this would come to light one day? How should I feel now? Hate, love, indifference? Should I carry on with my life without changing anything, or seek for my true identity, in the memory of my biological parents that lie hidden in the cold soil of another country, just because that's what other people wanted? Should I do something to appease their souls?"

Her thoughts were suddenly interrupted by Helga's cries. Although she wanted to be left alone today and make up her mind, upon hearing her daughter's voice, she leapt to her feet and grabbed the baby in her arms to kiss and talk to her.

"I'm sorry, Mrs. Anna, but she kept asking for you. I couldn't do otherwise."

"You did the right thing, Frieda. Alright. I'll spend some time with her. Prepare her for a walk."

During their walk, Anna felt calmer. She had to think with a cool head and decide what her reaction would be. For an instant, her gaze fell on Helga, who was playing happily in her pram. Without realising it, her mind scurried back to the past, a distant past that she wasn't allowed to live.

There, in the beautiful sun-drenched town by the sea, in the spring of 1943, a young, well-dressed lady had just got out of the house, pushing a wooden pram, where her only daughter was playing and laughing. As she looked at her, she felt on top of the world…The smile of this two-month-old girl made her forget the hard situation her country was going through.

This little creature seemed so familiar to Anna. She didn't know her name, but she felt it part of herself. Still, this young mother seemed completely unknown to her. Suddenly, after a few minutes, the sky went dark, and there were some voices and gunshots. Then, the image instantly changed. The mother vanished and the wooden pram slipped down the road, with the baby crying and lifting its little hands, in search of its mother.

Scared out of her wits, Anna screamed, which startled little Helga and made her cry. She picked her up straight away.

"What am I doing?" she wondered. "What if all this situation affects Helga? Maybe Sarah's right about asking me to leave my family out of this."

She walked further into the park, holding her daughter, and sat on a bench.

"I have to get over this quickly. I have to find a solution to this nightmare. My personal tragedy must not affect Helga and Adolf. Mrs. Andrea is right. I should talk to my mother first, sort this out, face up to the truth, and find out who I am. My mother, Mrs. Bird, loves me dearly, and I think she will tell me the truth. She will help me overcome this obstacle. After all, she wasn't to blame for that heinous crime against my real parents. She herself had a close shave and she brought me up in the best possible way. She may even help me find my parents if she's kept their names or any other information. Why didn't my father, who worked in the administration, try to help them? Even if he didn't, did he keep their names? I shouldn't let myself be tormented by all these thoughts and nightmares. I'd better make up my mind and speak to my mother. Sarah's right, after all…"

When she calmed down, Anna went back inside, where Adolf was waiting for her. This time, he felt much better seeing his wife holding the baby. After so many days of denial, Anna gave him a tender hug as she used to, which made her keep herself to herself. Adolf, affectionate as always, threw his arms around her and said:

"I don't know what's the matter with you, darling. I can understand your reactions, and I'm willing to help you sort out any problem. I'm not pushing you at all. I don't know how serious your problem is. I'm here by your side and always will be. No matter what it is, I hope you'll overcome it soon. It will do us good, especially Helga."

Kissing and smiling at him, Anna self-assuredly went up to her room, holding Helga.

CHAPTER TWELVE

Anna had made up her mind. She would speak to her mother right away. This dark chapter of her life should close as soon as possible. She couldn't put up with that nightmare that haunted her from such a tender age. She had decided not to say anything to Adolf. She would hide this truth from him as it didn't concern him. Besides, she didn't want him to know that she was of Jewish descent. She feared that he would see all this in a different, less favourable light because of his father's story.

On the other hand, though, Adolf's love of her and her beautiful country might do them good. Maybe she would tell him later. First, she would have to find her own identity, and for the time being, the only person who could help her was her mother—if Sarah had told her the truth, that is, and if her mother admitted to it.

The following morning, as soon as Adolf left for the uni, Anna got ready to visit her mother. It seemed that her encounter with aunt Greta's friend had radically changed Anna's behaviour, boosting her confidence. She wasn't afraid to face the truth, no matter how harsh. Today, she felt strong enough to confront her mother on this subject, as if she were a different person.

She called her mother to inform her that she needed to see her about something serious that had come up.

"What's going on, sweetheart? What's so serious at this time of day? Is it to do with Adolf? Helga? I'm really worried now."

"No, mum, no. It has to do with you. Adolf and Helga are doing great."

"Alright. I'll be waiting for you. Do you want me to come over?"

"No. I'll catch a taxi."

After a while, she walked into her paternal house with aplomb, ready to find out and confront the biggest truth of her life.

"Good morning, mother."

"Good morning, love. Come on in. What's the matter? You worried me to death. Come, take a seat and tell me. Shall I make some tea?"

"No. I will," said Anna and headed for the kitchen.

"Well, my beloved mother, I remember, seated on this very sofa, I once told you about my love affair with Adolf. Back then, you reacted like a normal mother."

She came up to her, held Mrs. Bird's hands, and taking a deep breath, she continued:

"Dear Mrs. Bird, my beloved mother, I want you to let me speak without interrupting me—unless, of course, you don't feel well. First of all, I want to thank you for giving me such an upbringing with principles and values. Of course, I barely knew my father, Hans. I don't remember him, but I'm immensely grateful to you."

"What's going on, sweetheart? Why are you saying all this to me?" her mother interrupted her abruptly.

"Mum…please, I asked you not to interrupt me. When I kept my affair with Adolf under wraps, I remember you telling me that we had no secrets. Actually, you told me you had never kept anything secret from me, that's why I shouldn't keep anything secret from you. Then, I told you how I felt for Adolf, and you hesitantly gave me your blessings."

"But…what kind of secrets are you talking about? I…"

"Please, mum. I didn't come here to interrogate you. You're my mother, and I owe you my life, right?"

Mrs. Bird's hands started to shake inside her daughter's sweaty palms.

"Anna, my only daughter, I want you to know that there are certain things in life that shouldn't be said if they are to cause any harm. Of course, I haven't yet understood what you're referring to."

"Mum, I want you to know that I fought hard to make the decision to talk to you. I strove to understand if a lie told so as not to cause any harm is better than truth with all its consequences."

Having realised what her daughter was talking about, Anna's mother was unable to keep her tears in check as she held her in her arms. Besides, her daughter's composure scared her even more. Anna let her cry as she held her still in her embrace. After a while, Mrs. Bird wiped her tears and, gaining her composure as a veritable German, she looked her straight in the eyes and said:

"My beloved daughter, if you allow me to call you like this, I want you to stop here. I want to continue this story. Of course, you're right about all this while I'm responsible for what happened in your life, but I want you to listen to me. For me, whatever happens after this conversation today, you are and always will be my beautiful little girl, my whole life. Your father and I swore to take this secret to our grave the moment we decided to keep you. I don't know how you found out—obviously from your father's circle. I want you to know that the moment I heard your cries in that abandoned house, I felt something wake up inside: my maternal instinct that I would never have felt otherwise."

The following day, when we realised the crime that was committed, your father pulled some strings to save your parents. Unfortunately, he didn't make it. The ruthless S-S official was intransigent, saying that he was forced to carry out the strict order he had been given. Actually, he even went so far as to threaten your father.

"Then, we made the big decision to save you, and, as they were searching for you in the civil register, we had no option, but to hide you. Your father then asked to be transferred to Berlin, where we returned two months later. Of course, thanks to our connections, we made sure to change all your birth documents, so we presented you as our own child. That's all…"

That moment, after her mother's apologetic stance, Anna shut the old woman's mouth and told her:

"Stop, my dear mummy. Don't say anything else. I don't want any more pain for us both. I still consider you my mother and thank you for saving my life. I don't know if what I've just learnt will do me good or harm in my life, but I want to tell you once again how much I love you. There's something else I want to say as well: The person who revealed all this to me didn't do it to harm me; she just happened to get her own identity forged as well. I won't tell you who that person is, though. They know you quite well, but probably you don't or can't even remember."

"You see how calmly we're talking about mine as well as my parents' tragedy, and maybe this strikes you as odd. After the first shock, I cried my eyes out, I got so hurt and said it'd be better now if I had died back then, together with my father and mother, but the existence of my beloved daughter gave me the strength to get over it. I want you to know that I love you just as much as I used to, and I'll always be by your side. What I found strange, though, is that this person kept repeating to me not to tell Adolf, which really got me thinking. That person is so strange and hurt, mummy."

"You said this person has a parallel story to yours and is from the same country where you were born?"

"Please allow me not to reveal this, Mrs. Bird, as this person asked me not to. Now I don't want Adolf or anyone else to find out anything. I also want you to help me learn more about my parents, although this must be really difficult. Who would ever have thought that our honeymoon would be in my own country last summer…?" Anna faltered.

The way she spoke to her mother about this tragedy brought peace of mind. Now that Mrs. Bird had made things clear, Anna felt the need to search for her real identity.

After she asked her to stay for lunch, her mother said:

"Never forget this, my love: This war, the worst war humankind ever knew, left behind only wounds and millions of innocent victims. And it was my own country that waged this war. As you can see, Germany is also divided after the harsh punishment of the bombings. There's something else I want you to know: In our life, we're often forced to do certain things we shouldn't and keep secrets for a good cause. Of course, lying can only cause harm to our souls, but—believe me, my dear!—those cries I heard that tragic day led me to do what I did, and I don't regret it. I still believe I gave life to you as well as myself. I needed to give meaning to my life and muster up the courage to raise you in the best possible way. As for your real parents, if they could see you from where they are, I think they would feel confident that their only daughter is growing up in a peaceful environment. The only thing you can blame me for is keeping this secret and never sharing it with you. The only reason behind this is fear for both you and me. Your father, Hans, wanted to tell you the truth when you grew up, but I didn't agree. On many occasions, life has different designs. You may run into such situations in your life, where you'll have to make some hard and unpleasant decisions. You have a beautiful daughter, the seed of love of you and the man you adore. Love and take care of her like I did, even if you are forced to keep a secret from her at some point. This is my advice, and make sure you never forget it. Considering the horror of the war back then, I feel proud that I saved the life of a tiny human being and made it part of my life."

Relieved by what she heard, Anna spontaneously hugged her mother and kissed her, and after assuring her that she was and always would be her favourite mother, she apologised for not staying for lunch and left. She had mixed feelings about her new life, but she was determined not to stop here. She would look into the matter. She left her mother's place with some questions on her mind and with a colder heart.

Day by day, Anna began to realise her new life, but tried not to show her inner change as it was really hard to handle at this tender age. Her mother's stance was really helpful, and Anna felt somewhat relieved and secure in Mrs. Andrea's company. Whatever that strange woman had revealed to her was absolutely true, so she couldn't, but trust her.

After a few days, she called her to do some catching-up and thank her. She wanted to tell her that her new identity didn't cause her any harm, and they would soon meet again. Sarah sounded content and repeated that Anna could count on her.

Anna's life got back to normal, but now she had some unfinished business, a sacred obligation—to look for her parents, who had met an untimely end. That would be her own tribute to them. Still, there was a great obstacle she had to overcome: Adolf. Once again, she decided to trust Sarah on that score—she wouldn't tell him anything. She was convinced that she should count on her to find out.

Although he found Anna's change weird, Adolf kept some distance politely and with discretion. This surely had a positive effect on little Helga.

Anna had also made another important decision. She wouldn't share her big secret with Emma either, at least for the time being, as she didn't want to expose Sarah—she had promised not to do it, after all. Just like her mother, she preferred to keep this to herself, seeing it as a personal tragedy she had to carry on her shoulders to the bitter end. Maybe later, she would trust only Helga when she grew up. She didn't want to act like Mrs. Bird. She would tell her daughter about her real grandmother and grandfather, her mother's distant, but true origins, and about that beautiful warm place where she was born as well as the tragedy that followed.

When she was home alone before Helga woke up in the mornings, she started poring over her books in her library. Now, apart from 'Medea,' she studied other things too. Even belatedly, she wanted to learn as much as she could about her lost country. She loved it as a foreign place. Greece was the country Adolf adored as well! It was the place that taught the world the principles of philosophy and virtue. The country that gave birth to democracy, which her own country now enjoyed after a period of harsh dictatorship that drowned the world and her real parents in blood.

This morning, after she called Emma to congratulate her on earning her degree, Anna asked her to come over to her place to talk. No longer stressed or tired, Emma agreed to see her, and after an hour, the two old classmates and cordial friends were sitting in the living room, sipping the hot coffee Frieda made.

"Well, my dear friend, I have to tell you how happy I am that you earned your degree. I want you to know that I'll always feel a void deep within as I'd like to be in your position. My dreams were interrupted by love and family."

"I understand, my dear Anna. Although all this came a bit early, you were very lucky as for the rest of your life; you'll have by your side a man and a scientist who loves you dearly and can support and help you with any obstacle you may run into. I have to see what I'm going to do in my life. You see, after you left that second row in the amphitheatre, I was left alone…"

"Since there are no secrets between us, my dear Emma, will you tell your best friend if there's anything else in your life?"

"Well, you'd be the first one to know if there was something else. As you said, we mustn't keep secrets, so I'll remind you last time we met. It was a long time ago but since I have a strong memory, let me tell you that you were quite upset. When we spoke on the phone, you sounded preoccupied. Something serious must have been going on. So are you keeping secrets from me? Is anything the matter with Adolf? Could I help in any way?"

"No, no, it's not serious. It's one of these things that come and go easily," Anna hastened to reply, unable to hide her agitation that flashed across her face. Of course, this didn't go unnoticed.

"Is it to do with your mother? To the best of my memory, she had her objections to your marriage."

"No, no," Anna repeated. "Let's not discuss all this. It was trivial. Tell me, what are you going to do now that you've completed your studies? Shall I tell you something that will surely make you happy?"

"Yes, what?"

"The other day, Adolf told me that you were one of the very best students—not because you're my best friend. Actually, he's going to suggest that you pursue an academic career if that's what you want. He's more than willing to help you. To be frank, he asked me not to tell you anything, but I wanted to be the first to tell you this, even if Adolf gets angry!"

Upon hearing this, Emma leapt to her feet, threw her arms around her friend, and thanked her with a broad smile.

"You can't imagine what this means to me, my dear Anna! I was sort of disappointed. I feared I wouldn't find a job. Thanks a lot! I'll accept this offer without thinking twice. Who wouldn't like to work with him, after all?"

"That's great! I'm so glad! Still, don't give away our secret!" said Anna laughingly.

"Tell me what you're up to, apart from taking care of your husband and daughter… Sorry! I didn't ask about Helga. She must have grown into a beautiful baby!"

"She's doing great! She's growing up and she's a nice baby girl! I've got news for you! Do you remember we went on holiday to that beautiful country, Greece, last summer? I mean myself and Adolf. We had such a good time!"

"Sure I know that, my dear. I think you told me. How come you remembered it again?"

"Well, Adolf and I are thinking of going there again. After all, he promised to do that. He will learn about the summer performances in the ancient Greek theatres and, if my favourite tragedy 'Medea'—I suppose you remember it—is playing, we'll attend it! I've read so much about this country. Apart from its capital city Athens and its wonderful islands, it also boasts a great north city. It's called Salonica. I really want to visit it. It's by the coast, with a nice tower by the sea. That's its landmark. From what I've read, its people are really hospitable, simple, and kindhearted."

"Don't speak so fast! You'll choke on your food!" Emma cut in. "I see this country enchanted you! I'd love to visit it myself!"

"It's never too late, my dear. I promise we'll go there, the two of us, one day, and I'll be the one to show you around. I read about its history and its people every day. I read somewhere that it's the country with the most hospitable people, so much so that in its mythology there is a god that symbolised hospitality."

"Alright, alright! I gather this country has found yet another fan, apart from the professor. I think Adolf loves you so much that he'll do whatever you ask for—and you're really lucky on that score!"

Anna seemed to be irritated upon hearing the word 'lucky.'

"Lucky? I don't know who's lucky and unlucky in this life, my dear Emma. This notion is open to debate! Many times, some things look different."

"What are you talking about, girlie? You're dropping hints again. Are you hiding something from me?"

"No, my dear. Er…well…I just meant that…today, someone might be lucky and all of a sudden, their life may be turned upside down. I'm speaking in general. I mean that… maybe in the future you'll be lucky and get a position like that of Adolf, and I'll be there to admire you. That's all I wanted to tell you."

"Well, I agree with you," replied Emma in puzzlement.

After a few minutes, Helga's cries interrupted them.

Emma rose from her seat, hugged Helga, kissed her, and said:

"My sweet little Helga, you've grown up! You're such a good girl! I love you so much!" After playing with her for some time, she made to leave—just as Adolf arrived.

"What a surprise! I get to see the two young classmates of the second row back together again!" he exclaimed as soon as he saw them, but first, he spread his arms open to hug his precious daughter.

"Good morning, professor. I'm so glad to see you!"

"Emma, let's dispense with this 'professor' thing. You know my name quite well. In a short while, we may be colleagues. Actually, right now, in my own house, I recommend that you apply to the university, and I'll back you up. You surely deserve it, and the uni needs young people like you." As he saw how awkward Anna felt, he continued: "Of course, I'd love to see both of you at the uni, but I preferred to have my beloved wife by my side, not just for a few hours, but for the rest of my life." At the sound of his words, Anna's face lit up and Emma smiled.

Holding Helga, he went up to his wife to greet his future colleague.

"See you soon, Emma. Of course, your friend will be there too, so that she won't start getting any silly ideas!"

"Sure I'll be there!" exclaimed Anna laughingly.

CHAPTER THIRTEEN

As days went by, Anna's mind often scurried back to those first two months of her life. Without realising it, she started keeping herself to herself again, plunging into thoughts. She had also stopped seeing her mother very often. When it dawned on her that they had drifted apart, she called her, but without feeling joy like before. The first thing she did was come up with some excuses. Mrs. Bird blamed herself for this change of behaviour.She was sometimes consumed with guilt, not because she had changed Anna's identity, but because she hadn't told her the truth. She wanted that little baby she had found in the abandoned house to live a happy life after being violently snatched away from her parents. She thought she had actually given life to two people. That's what she thought was the right thing to do—and she wouldn't stop seeing it that way.

Sometimes, Mrs. Bird felt she was all alone in life. She was so scared. This morning, as her daughter hadn't communicated with her for almost a week, she decided to visit her unexpectedly. Anna was really surprised to see her.

"Morning, mother! What a pleasant surprise! Come in. Is something the matter?" asked Anna when she saw her and threw herself into her arms.

Her daughter's tender embrace gave Mrs. Bird such a relief, brushing off the fear that had overwhelmed her soul. Anna felt that straight away. She held her tightly and pulled her to the big sofa in the living room.

"Mum, please take a seat. As I see what's going on with you, I want you to know how much I love you. Nothing's changed, but I had to recover or, rather, pretend to be alright in front of others."

"So that means you're not really well, my child?" asked her mother in a quivering voice.

"Mum, you have to understand that what I went through wasn't simple. It was a hurricane, an earthquake that shook my soul. I must get over it soon as my life's been thrown out of whack. The other day, when I saw Emma, I almost let the cat out of the bag. I have the house chores, taking care of Helga and Adolf. Can you imagine how much effort I have to put in to face all this now?"

Hearing her only daughter speak so maturely, Mrs. Bird stared deep into her eyes and said:

"Honey, I'm so sorry about this story. I want you to forgive me for what I did. The truth is, I had decided not to share my secret with you as I thought this would be better for you, but now I see I was wrong. The truth, no matter how harsh, is always better than lies. I also want you to forgive your father, Hans, who couldn't save your parents. And don't you ever think that we didn't try to save them and seized the opportunity to have the child we'd always dreamt of. Don't you ever forget that you're my whole life?"

"Over the last days, my heart's been beating in a strange way. I want to have a peaceful death with no guilt. When I go to bed at night, I hear voices, as if they're judging me. I'm afraid I won't make it in the end."

"What are you talking about, mummy? Have you been to the doctor? Why didn't you tell me straight away? Maybe now you should think seriously about moving in with me."

"No, we've been over this. I feel great at my place, I have my best friend there, and we take care of each other. You know who I mean. Well, I have a burden on my chest, and it comes and goes. I'll gradually get over it."

"I don't want you to experience any problems. I'll love you forever like I used to. You brought me up; you gave me your life."

But Mrs. Bird couldn't take all this anymore. The moment she decided to take that baby with her, forging Anna's identity, she was sure her secret would never be revealed as only she and her husband knew it. Back then, he could change all the baby's details, so after his wife had been away for nine months, they both turned up in Berlin with a baby, whom she had given birth to in Greece.

But it wasn't only this feeling of sadness that had an impact on her health. It was an inexplicable rage over the person who had revealed her secret and wreaked havoc with their peaceful lives...

"My girl, I've come here today to ask you who told you all this. I think I'm entitled to know. And you must tell me, darling, right?"

Her mother's unusual tone of voice seemed to irritate Anna.

"Mum, what came over you? I find it strange that you ask me to do that in such a tone. Let me remind you that I pleaded with you not to do it from the start. I told you I wouldn't reveal the name of that person. After all, what difference does it make now since what I was told is true? I could be livid and aggressive, but as you saw, I kept my wits about me and thanked you for saving my life, although I found out I had been living a lie all these years."

"You're right, sweetheart. Many times, lying is more convenient than telling the truth. Maybe I desired to have a baby that led me to this act. Maybe this truth that sneaked up on me is my biggest punishment. And this remorse inside my brain is here to take my life away."

"Remorse? What remorse, mother? I've already forgiven you…"

"I don't know what this remorse is, my daughter, but when it comes, it feels so bad, you'd rather die."

"Come on. You have no reason to feel like that. Let's change the subject. I promise to visit you more often. Will you be staying for lunch? Helga will be happy to see you…"

"No, I'm leaving. I came only for you. Kiss her."

Anna had never seen her mother in this condition, but she herself felt different deep within. Without understanding why she had become harder. "What's this remorse Mrs. Bird mentioned?" she wondered. "I'll ask Adolf in the afternoon. He surely knows."

At lunchtime, unable to wait any longer, Anna asked him out of curiosity:

"Darling, what's remorse?"

"Where did that come from?" asked Adolf.

"Er…well…I read it somewhere and I didn't get it."

"Alright. After lunch, we'll go to the library and, if you're not tired, I'll analyse another great work, another tragedy, which is related to this word." In a while, after taking a book out of a drawer, he began:

"Well, this book describes another tragic story set in the country you loved and spent your holiday in last summer. After the end of the victorious war waged by this country in antiquity, its leader comes back to find his wife, with whom he had a son, Orestes, with her lover. Then, they both kill the king. When the son finds out, he too murders his mother and her lover to avenge himself. After this act, he ran hither and thither, consumed with some frenzied inner voices that kept reminding him of his abominable deed. As he couldn't find closure, he was tried by the supreme court, which acquitted him. Yet, despite this, he couldn't spare himself his torturous remorse. These inner voices and thoughts are what we call remorse or guilt, but why are you racking your innocent brain with all this? You're so young and there are so many beautiful things for you to do to make your life prettier!"

"Ah, I get it now!" said Anna. "Is there a chance that someone may never be able to get rid of their remorse?"

"Yes, there is. You see, those bright minds came up with timeless works. Let's get some rest now, my dear student. Helga needs us."

When Adolf went upstairs, Anna stayed in the office.

"So that's what remorse is all about," she thought. "That's what haunts Mrs. Bird and won't let her be. And, if remorse can drive someone crazy, what can it do to all those who executed so many innocent people during the war? What can remorse do to that criminal who had my parents killed for no apparent reason and denied me their presence before I even saw the light of day? Is he still alive? Will he feel guilty for his crimes?" If only she could find him and ask him why he had committed that crime, and tell him that story she had just heard from the professor...

"Maybe Sarah," she thought. Maybe she could help her. Everything she had told her was true. Why shouldn't Anna trust her now?

"I'll call her tomorrow," she thought. "After all, I owe her a visit. I will thank her for changing my life and making me stronger. Is it true what they say about the truth making you stronger, no matter how bitter and harsh?"

CHAPTER FOURTEEN

The next morning, Anna called Sarah. After her last conversation with her mother, she felt the irrepressible need to talk to the old lady.

"Good morning, sweetheart. I was sure you'd call me one day."

"Morning, my dear Sarah. I felt the need to see you and have a chat. First of all, I want to ask you a few things, but I think you want to tell me more anyway."

"Alright. Don't panic. I'm waiting for you today. How's your little doll?"

"She and Adolf are fine, Sarah. I hope you don't mind my calling you by your first name. I consider you my friend."

"Of course, my dear Anna! I suppose you have a lot to tell me. I'm waiting. Are you coming over today?"

"I'll be there in an hour. I have a few questions to pose and something to ask you for."

In an hour, the two women were seated on the couch in Mrs. Andrea's small and uncomfortable living room. Standing on her own two feet, Anna thanked her friend and told her exactly what she had discussed with her mother and that she had kept her promise. Touched, but content, Sarah thanked her for trusting her.

"From now on, Anna, for as long as I live, I'll stand by you as your best friend. There are many things I'd like to tell you, but I'll stick to what I've already told you. You've found out about your life and now you must carry on with it. I see you're quite calm in relation to the tragic story of your life, and you shouldn't get overwhelmed with more. You see, sometimes life has so much in store for us, either pleasant or unpleasant — things we can't even imagine!"

"You scare me again, my dear Sarah! I came here to learn more as I'm sure you're hiding things. No matter how much it cost me, this story helped me grow strong and I think I can cope with more. That's why there's something I want to ask for."

"Tell me, sweetheart."

"My mother told me that my father, thanks to his high-ranking post, tried to release my parents when he found me in that place. Yet, the officer was harsh and adamant. Then, after he forged my identity, my parents disappeared without a trace. Besides, from what my mother told me, I realised she didn't really want to tell me what became of my parents; she just kept talking about herself and me, but I want to search and find. To be frank, I pretended to be thankful to her for saving my life, but day by day, I come to realise what an immoral thing she and Hans did. Maybe she lied to me about my parents. Since she did such a thing and lived in this lie all these years, why couldn't she tell yet another lie?

"I don't want to find out how they died, but since I had a discussion with Adolf about human remorse, I feel the need to discover if those who murdered them feel guilty."

Upon hearing Anna's last words, Sarah leapt to her feet and, trying to hide her agitation, she told her:

"No, no, my dear! You're hankering after the moon. Just leave all this behind. All those horrible things that happened back then should be a thing of the past. You must carry on with your life as you're at a tender age and the future lies ahead. I'll try digging into the clues I collected while working at the Ministry, and I may find something by pulling a few strings. But, even if you find these criminals, what will you be able to do?"

"Maybe I'll reveal all this to Adolf, who could find something if he uses his father's connections. He used to serve that regime back then. That will be my way to pay tribute to their memory, but I saw you got upset earlier, just like you did the first time we talked. Are you hiding something from me, something to do with my parents this time?"

"No. Well…I always get upset when I'm talking about that period. You see, I relive my own tragic story. Don't pay any attention. Ever since I met you, I've sworn to myself to help you get over all these lies. I hope your parents' souls will find salvation. As I told you before, I don't want you to say anything to Adolf.

"His father was a high-ranking official, and I don't know how he would react if he found out you're a Jew. Of course, he doesn't seem to be such a man, but I have to be cautious after what I've been through in my life."

"Alright. I'll do exactly what I promised and wait for your help."

After their short conversation, Anna began to feel intimate with her new friend.

On her way back home, she looked calm after Sarah told her she was more than eager to help. What aroused her suspicions was Sarah's insistence that she not talk to Adolf. Obviously, she had her own reasons. Anna wouldn't speak to Adolf for the time being; she had Mrs. Bird's health condition to deal with. She was really worried. The two women had drifted apart, it was true. Still, she had to care for her, ignoring her mother's unprecedented reactions the previous day.

"I have to spend more time with Helga too," she thought as she walked into her place. "I think I've neglected her. Tomorrow, I'll devote the whole day to my little princess."

A while later, Adolf came home. He was so happy to see Anna in high spirits.

"Alright with remorse?" he asked her with a smile. "Have we learnt this chapter?"

"Yes, very well. How did that cross your mind, darling?"

"Ah…well…because it's still fresh. You know what? I hope your soul will never be consumed with torturous images and thoughts."

"Have you ever felt guilty in your life?" Anna asked him spontaneously.

"Me? No… at least up to now. In order to feel guilty, you must have committed something serious at the expense of others or yourself."

"I'm asking you, honey, because your father served as a high-ranking official during the war. As you know better than me, all sorts of hideous crimes are committed during the war."

"I agree, but you should know people carry out orders in wartime, and many times innocent people get killed on both sides. On the other hand, why are we raking over the ashes now? After such a long time, all this has gone down in history. I didn't want to follow my father's career. I hate wars because innocent civilians are killed. From an early age, I was entranced by civilisation and philosophy. That's what helped me forget the horror of the war and its crimes, but let's drop this boring subject, please! It's no good for either of us!"

"You're right. I don't know what came over me. I'm sorry. Let's drop it."

Over the following days, Anna spent most of her time with Helga. After all, she had been through, she felt closer to her baby now. She also made time for her mother, mainly because of her health issues. She wanted to show her how much she still cared for her, despite Mrs. Bird's insistence that she not dig into her life.

CHAPTER FIFTEEN

Spring came earlier this year. The weather was looking up day by day, and the green landscape made Berlin so much prettier. Nature's beauty, though, did not affect Anna. On the one hand, all these events that had dramatically changed her life had helped her mature, but an indeterminate sense of fear nestled in her soul as if something bad was going to happen. This made her nervous and try as she might, she couldn't hide her agitation. Besides, although she tried to contact her mother regularly, she felt something had cracked inside. Her mind was stuck on that story that had turned her life upside down. Sarah's last words — she called her every day—her mother's aggressiveness, and the fact that Mrs. Bird didn't visit her again made Anna keep herself to herself. In her own private place, her library, she spent hours on end, searching for and studying books on her new country — or rather her only country. The country she had never known in any depth.

Adolf seemed to watch her discreetly. It had dawned on him that something wasn't quite right with his wife; it could be something serious, but he didn't want to push her or tease anything out of her. Maybe the fact that he had a soft spot for her made him keep his distance and wait until she decided to speak to him.

The summer was drawing near. Helga had grown up and was a quiet, obedient, and well-mannered child. She took after Adolf character-wise, and this really pleased him, although he didn't let it show. In a few days, the University would break up for the summer holidays, and Adolf couldn't wait to spend time with his loved ones. He had already made plans for their summer vacations. This time, Helga would join them.

However, just as he was about to announce his proposal to Anna, an unexpected phone call forced him to put it on the back-burner. Aunt Greta was rushed into hospital in a serious condition. Adolf and Anna dashed there to see her. For Adolf, Aunt Greta was his only relative still alive.

Before they entered Aunt Greta's hospital ward, her doctor broke the news to Adolf: her health condition was critical. After a few minutes, Adolf and Anna stood over her bed. As soon as she saw them, she cracked a smile and slowly reached out to hold her nephew's hand. Her low voice showed how weak she felt.

"Welcome to my new room, my children. It's a bit smaller than my own house, but I'll manage," she said smilingly.

"What are you talking about, my dear aunt?" Adolf asked her.

"We're here by your side. As the doctor said, you'll be up and about soon."

"My dear children, thanks for coming over to see me, but deep down, I know what's going to happen to me far better than the doctors," aunt Greta whispered with a bitter smile on her face. "Sit here close to me. I'll tell you a few things before I leave. I want to say that I have no complaints. I lived on my own for years. I never managed to raise my own family, so after my brother and his wife's death, I devoted my life to taking care of you, Adolf. That's why I considered you to be my own child. It was as if I had adopted you."

Upon hearing this, Anna bowed her head, holding Aunt Greta's hands. Then, she said:

"Aunt Greta, your words have really moved me to tears. This horrible war seems to have claimed so many lives on both sides, bringing misery to those left behind, but we're here now, by your side, and we won't leave you alone. The doctor informed us earlier that you're out of harm's way and you'll soon recover."

"My darling, my dear Anna, I want you to know that I'm so glad to see you. When I learnt you were my son's wife, I was over the moon. I leave him in your hands to raise Helga in the best possible way, have more children, and live your whole life happily. Don't tell me anything else. Adolf, when I'm gone, everything I have will be yours. I've already transferred my small fortune to you. The notary has my will. Now please leave me alone. I want to rest for a while. Kiss my little girl, and never forget what I told you. Always love each other and stick together.

"Ah! My dear Anna, I forgot to tell you that Mrs. Andrea — you know, my friend you met at my place a while ago — really liked you and said she'd be there if you need anything."

Upon hearing that name, Anna cracked a bitter smile as she walked out of the ward.

On their way back inside the car, they were both silents. They were sad and feared Aunt Greta would soon pass away. Adolf spent the rest of the day contacting the hospital.

Two days later, the news of her death was announced. As he always had a cool head, Adolf discreetly carried through the funeral procedures. After all, his aunt had very few friends and acquaintances. On Anna's side, her mother, Mrs. Bird, and Sarah attended. Mrs. Andrea looked very sad as she had lost her best friend. Of course, she had been replaced by her new friend, young Anna. They only exchanged formalities, and at some point, Anna whispered she would call her as soon as she was left alone at home.

A month later, Adolf decided not to miss out on their summer holiday because of his aunt's death and announced to Anna that he was thinking of going to a nice resort in Southern Spain together with Helga and Anna. Still, his wife had other things on her plate.

"That's a great idea, my love, having Helga with us, but, you know, I want to ask you a favour and I think you won't say no."

"You know I never say no to you. I'm all ears!"

"Well…let's go back to Greece to spend our summer holiday. I had such a great time last year. I was so entranced that I didn't get my fill! I've read so much about this country, and I feel I adore it already…Of course, you are to blame for this because you taught me about this place through your lessons. Don't forget that last year you promised to find out about the performances that will be held at the ancient theatres, more specifically 'Medea'…"

"Alright, alright, my love. You needn't say anything more. Of course, we'll go there again! And I'm going to keep my promise: I'll find out about the performances tomorrow."

Anna spontaneously threw herself into his arms.

"Thank you so much! I'll start packing up! One last favour when we get there."

"Accepted," replied Adolf laughingly. He couldn't, but notice that Anna was smiling so joyfully after such a long time.

In a few days, father, mother, and daughter flew south. This time, though, they didn't feel the same. Adolf was joyful as he saw bliss in Anna's eyes, unable to discern the melancholy deep inside them. It was also that little creature that made him twice as happy. Anna tried to pretend so as not to let her stress, agony, and indeterminate fear show. Two days before, she had seen Sarah, told her about the trip, and asked her for all the clues she knew as to the place where she was born and her paternal house. If she went to the place where her father Hans lived, she might find her own since it was right beside it. If it was still standing, that is…

Sarah was opposed to that as she feared Adolf might find out, but Anna, knowing she had a soft spot for her, reassured her, saying she would make it. She also promised this would be the only thing she would handle on her own. She had it all planned in her head for quite some time. On the second day, they saw a performance at the ancient theatre and then enjoyed the sea on one of the beautiful islands. Once they were there, three days later, she would ask Adolf to go to her hometown, Salonica.

Helga, who was a lilliputian lady by now, was taciturn, but her eyes watched everything around her. She was a living doll that, as she grew up, looked more and more like her father.

Helga attended tonight's performance like a grownup. She didn't understand anything, but Adolf and Anna didn't understand the language, either. However, he made sure to remind Anna of the plot and themes of 'Medea,' which had left its indelible mark on Anna.

The whole scenery and grandiosity of this renowned theatre mattered as much as the play itself.

The next day, they caught the morning plane for the Knights' beautiful Island, as it was called. The weather was fantastic and little Helga was thrilled about the sea and the sun. Anna's mind, though, was elsewhere. Ever since she set foot in Greece, she had been trying to seize the opportunity to ask Adolf for what she was there for.

At some point, on their second day on the island, holding a map, she told him spontaneously:

"Darling, will you do me one last favour?"

"I told you, sweetheart. I'll do whatever you want."

"Well, as I said, I've read a lot about this country and there's another place I'd like to visit before we leave."

"What crossed your mind again?"

"I'll tell you, but remember you promised me, right?"

"Sure! And I answer before I even hear what it's about."

"Well, I want to go to another beautiful city for a couple of days. It's in the north. I mean Salonica. It's a city by the coast. Are we going, darling?"

"Why d'you ask? Can I say no?" replied Adolf with a smile. "Well, I only worry about Helga. Maybe she'll get tired. Look what a great time she's having here…"

"Well, I understand that. You're right. Still, we have so many years and journeys ahead of us…"

Adolf interrupted her: "Therefore, we're leaving for this beautiful city, Salonica, tomorrow, alright?"

Anna was so excited that she threw herself into his arms and kissed him.

The next morning, after they stopped over in Athens, half an hour later, they landed in that beautiful northern city, which was more impoverished than the capital, still bearing the marks of the war and the period of Occupation. Adolf wasn't really excited at what he saw there, but Anna was gripped by a strange feeling the moment she set foot in the city. Try as she might, she couldn't hide that from Adolf. Once they settled in their hotel room, wasting no time, Anna went to the reception desk, asking for a light supper for Helga. As she couldn't wait to visit the area she was interested in, she asked how far it was from the hotel. Sarah hadn't given her many clues. Anna was so anxious to find her parents' place that she didn't mind letting the cat out of the bag. The only information she had was that the two houses were in the centre by the sea. When the receptionist gave her some directions, she placed her order and ran back to their room.

"Is everything OK?" asked Adolf.

"Yes, yes…Everything's fine."

Tired from their constant trips, Helga had dozed off in her father's arms. Stressed as she was, Anna held her beloved daughter, put her to bed, and without much thought, told Adolf in a steady and determined voice:

"Sweetheart, as we can't leave this room together, you'll stay here with your daughter as you don't look very excited to explore the city. I'll go out for a walk. I saw there's a beautiful beach right in front of the entrance." Before Adolf had the chance to say anything, she grabbed hold of her bag and dashed out of the room. He didn't have a clue what was going on with her.

As soon as she stepped out in the street, she felt relieved and completely free, as if she had been kept in captivity.

"I have to do everything in a flash. Adolf mustn't suspect anything," she thought as she quickened her gait. A rush of adrenaline made her heart pound.

After the elderly receptionist told her a few things about the area where Germany's Consulate was during Occupation, she started asking passersby, showing them a piece of paper where something was written in the local language, her parents' mother tongue. When she got the information she needed, she caught a cab, showing the driver's address.

During those ten minutes inside the taxi, she couldn't think of anything else. Her anxiety and stress wouldn't let her hear the driver's voice, as he repeated:

"We're here, madam."

As if in a daze, she stood before the old two-storey mansion. Signalling the driver to wait, she walked into the yard. The place was uninhabited. Still, Anna didn't mind that. She walked around the yard, trying to find her own place, based on her mother's information and poor description. What she saw was a derelict building. Her instinct told her that was the place she was looking for. Stepping on the ruins, she bent over to touch the stones. She was all alone right now. She wanted to cry and call out their names in case they heard her as she did back then, on that tragic day, when Mrs. Bird, fortunately, heard her. That outburst of emotion got that weight off her chest. Her greedy eyes tried to capture all those images, cherishing them deep within; nothing would ever pluck them away.

She saw little Anna, a scared girl by another name, crying her eyes out, unable to understand the unspeakable tragedy around her. She sat on a stone and, stroking her; she started whispering to herself:

"What would my life be like now if I had grown in this house, together with my beloved parents, if the war and those criminals who killed them hadn't taken them away from me? How different would the world be without wars..."

She leapt to her feet and, not minding soiling her clothes; she walked through the ruins on the off-chance of spotting that place where Mrs. Bird heard her cry for the first time — the moment that changed her life forever. Forever or until now? After a few minutes, as if snapping out of her deep slumber, she took one last look and headed for the taxi. She paid the driver and asked him to show her the way back. She wanted to walk, along with her favourite thoughts.

What she saw might not be her own house, but that's how she viewed it and she would cherish that image for the rest of her life.

When she got to the hotel, Helga was still asleep and Adolf exhausted as well, had shut his eyes beside his daughter. The noise awakened him, though. Having rehearsed her answer, Anna threw herself into his arms, thanking him for visiting this city. She told him he was right — it wasn't particularly interesting. As always, he planted a kiss on her cheek and asked no questions.

The next morning, after they got back to Athens, they flew to Berlin.

For Anna, that was the 'nicest' trip of her life.

CHAPTER SIXTEEN

That morning, Anna was in high spirits. She had come back from her holiday a couple of days before, Helga was still resting, and Adolf was getting ready for the new academic year. He also had some unfinished business concerning aunt Greta's death. Anna wouldn't call Sarah yet to tell her about her impressions. She wasn't in a hurry. She looked much calmer now. She only felt a little guilty for keeping her distance from her mother, Mrs. Bird. Her feelings hadn't changed — and they never would — after she visits that tragic city where they lived together. That's why she asked Adolf to visit her the next day. Anna was also worried about her mother's wellbeing after her last health issue.

The next morning, after she called her, she prepared Helga and they left after a while. She was going to her second paternal home. Still, they were in for a surprise. Mrs. Bird was not feeling well, which showed in the condition of her house.

"Mother, what's going on? The place is a mess! You don't look very well either. You're sick. Why didn't you call us?"

"Come, sit down. I'm fine," she pretended, trying to show that her condition wasn't very serious. She tried to give Helga a tight hug, but she didn't make it.

Adolf had her lie on the couch, and Anna sat next to her.

"Why all this, mum? Didn't we talk about that last time you came over? Didn't I tell you you weren't in very good condition? Didn't I ask you to stay with us so that we can take care of you?"

"Yes, you did and I refused as I can't change my habits after so many years. I want to stay here till I die. Maybe I'm not going to be a burden on you for much longer. My heart's grown weak, as the doctor said. He gave me some medication, telling me not to be sad as sadness harms the heart."

"Why would you be sad, Mrs. Bird? Unless you mean Anna's absence. As I've heard, she asked you to come over to our place, so that we can take care of you. I'm all for that!" Adolf said on the spot.

"Thank you both. No, my child, I'm not sad about Anna. On the contrary, I'm so happy that she married a man like you, Adolf, and I know she will live with love and security. Bear in mind, though that sometimes we carry some things we cherish and bring sorrow when faced with them. On the other hand, let's not talk about all this now. Tell me, did you go on holiday? Did you have a good time?"

"Ah! Mrs. Bird, this year, we went to the same place as last summer. Anna asked me to go to Greece again, but the three of us this time. She was so thrilled last summer, and probably I am to blame as I teach about this country at the uni," Adolf responded laughingly.

Upon hearing this, Mrs. Bird couldn't hide her agitation. Seeing this, Anna rose from her seat, changed the subject, and said, as she held Helga:

"Baby, this beautiful sweet lady is your grannie and I want you to know that she loves you as much as she loved me when I was that small. She's a little sick, but she'll soon be alright. Then, you'll play together and she'll tell you fairytales as she did to me."

But this intervention on Anna's part wasn't enough to shake stress and fear off her mother's face.

They didn't stay there for long. After Anna asked her once again to stay at their place, they said goodbye and left.

Early the next morning, when Adolf left for work, Anna called her mother. She wanted to make it clear that she was the one who asked for this journey as she wanted to see her country — more specifically, the city where she was born. She also meant to tell her that she would love her like her real mother. Still, Mrs. Bird had to understand that Anna's sacred duty was to look for those who had deprived her of her biological parents before she could make sense of the world.

Yet, after that fateful discovery, Mrs. Bird didn't have the strength to carry on with her life. Her remorse wouldn't let her be day and night. Anna could see that, but her mother's stubborn refusal wouldn't let her help her.

The academic year was in full swing and Adolf went about his everyday duties. Anna called her mother every single day as this was the only way she could show her she had forgiven her for what she had done. It wasn't so much the fact that she had concealed her identity as her act itself.

But it was also Sarah and Emma. Emma wanted to hear how Anna's holiday was. Sarah, her new friend, had opened her eyes to the truth — a half-truth. Anna thought Sarah was keeping other secrets as well. Secrets that must have had to do with what had happened to her parents and how she could make sense of all this. She believed that, when she discovered all this, her soul would probably calm down and she would be able to carry on with her life.

After a few days, she felt the need to call Sarah to have a chat and, if her research yielded some results, the two friends might meet up.

Sarah's voice at the other end of the line sounded a little weak, though.

"Good morning, my dear Sarah. It's Anna. You don't sound very well. Is anything the matter?"

"Yes, dear. I feel a bit tired. I've had breathing problems for years now since the war, but this year it's deteriorated. How are you doing? Was everything alright? I was anxious to know, but I didn't want to disturb you."

"I'm fine. Mum, Mrs. Bird, isn't feeling very well, and I'm really worried about her health condition. Now you're the second person I worry about. I'm coming over tomorrow to check on you. If you're in a position to listen to me, I'll tell you all about my trip to Greece. I don't want to push you; if you have any news, I'm more than eager to hear it."

The next day, when Adolf went to work, she left after asking Frieda to say she would be out shopping if Adolf called. Helga was used to Frieda's presence, and they both got on very well. After a while, Anna walked into the small flat.

"Good morning, my sweetest Sarah," she greeted her with a kiss. For her, Sarah was a very good friend.

"Welcome, beauty!" the woman responded in a weak voice. "Come, sit here with me to have a chat."

"Sure! But first, tell me how you're feeling. What did you tell me on the phone? I was really worried. It might sound a little bit odd, but I see you as a mother, although I barely know you. That's so ironic, isn't it? Deep in my soul, I have three mothers while, in fact, I have none!"

"Calm down, sweetheart. Tell me about your trip first."

"Ah…Well, that was the most beautiful trip I've ever had in my life."

"So you went there, you made, eh? Did you find anything?"

"Yes, we went there together. It seems that Adolf didn't suspect anything. Actually, he never says no, whatever I ask of him! Helga's presence played a role, of course, as I seized the opportunity to independently leave our hotel room. I found Mrs. Bird's house. It's in relatively good condition, but uninhabited. Next to it is another one that's in ruins. My instinct told me this was my parents' place, my own place. I stayed there amid the ruins for a while, crying and feeling a chapter of my life came to a close."

Moved, Sarah cradled her and said:

"Alright, honey. Now I think only a chapter in your life drew to a close back then. Now you can look ahead."

"That's right, Sarah. Only a chapter drew to a close back then. There's another one that needs to close. Then, I'll be able to shake off this darkness in my soul, and look at my life anew, together with my husband and daughter — if I finally make it, that is. Well, will you help me close this chapter?"

"You're in a hurry, my child. It's not that easy. I've collected some evidence, but this may further compound the situation. You know, all this time, I've thought whether we should rake over the ashes. I'm afraid, in the end, instead of healing the wounds, you may inflict new unbearable ones. Maybe we should stop here and make a new start."

Determined to see all this through to the end, Anna stared deep into Sarah's eyes and said:

"My beloved friend, I've sworn to myself to make it to the bitter end at all costs. I owe that to you as well as to my parents' souls. What did you say about new wounds?"

"Alright, alright. Calm down!" responded Sarah, breathing more and more heavily. "Give me a sec. I want to take my pills."

"I'm sorry, Sarah. It's my fault. Maybe my reactions affected you deeply."

"No, we're going to pick up where we left off. I'll lie on the couch for a while. I have more things to say. I won't hide anything as I see you're dead set on it."

Half an hour later, Sarah was much better. She held Anna's hand and continued:

"My sweet daughter, I understand the weight you've been carrying from an early age is unbearable. I just thought maybe you shouldn't carry any more of it."

"What d'you mean by that? Your words put me in mind of the first time we met before you told me the big truth. You dropped hints. Is there something else you've been hiding from me?"

"No, my dear Anna, I don't have enough evidence regarding your parents' fate. Still, I promise to find by sifting through some other friends' files. I simply mean the whole story is littered with bloodsheds and horror, and I wouldn't like to deal your sensitive soul yet another blow."

"Sarah, I need to say something about that. Ever since I started pondering all this, my heart has turned to stone and I see life so differently. Once again, I want to ask you why you think I mustn't seek Adolf's help. He loves me so much and always indulges me. He proved that last summer."

"No, we've ruled that out. Adolf must not find out your true identity. You don't know. Maybe it will disrupt your balance at home."

"Yes, but this has changed now and Adolf has nothing to do with such matters."

"No, I'm still scared. Please don't insist. I want to make sure I'll be the one to collect the evidence we're looking for. I pray to God to give me some more time as the thread of my life will be cut at some point."

"Haven't we talked about that already? Nothing will happen to you. I'll always be by your side. I'll call you every day."

"Thanks, my daughter. Before I depart from this world, I want you to know that which will happen soon—I'll give you all the clues I have, along with the ones I will gather. This time, as I won't be there for you, you must be strong to face the situations on your own."

"I think we'll be together for many, many years," said Anna with a smile, holding the woman's hand tenderly.

As she left Sarah's house, Anna felt relieved to have talked to her. She hopes to see all this through to the end were rekindled. She promised herself what she had sworn to Adolf when they met for the first time, looking him in the eyes: that they would be together to the bitter end...

CHAPTER SEVENTEEN

That year was drawing to a close. In the Krause's house, Anna's family lived a seemingly quiet everyday routine, away from the previous months' tension. She started spending more time with her daughter. As for Sarah and her mother, their health condition was looking up. Adolf tried to leave work earlier to spend more time with his wife and daughter. The only thing he had seen over the past days, though, was how badly he needed to be with Anna. Not that it was unpleasant, but sometimes he felt trapped and hamstrung. Still, he paid no mind.

Anna's mother, Mrs. Bird, was the one Anna was mostly worried about, although her condition was improving. She knew the old lady's mental condition better than anyone else; that's why she made sure to call her every single day.

Now that New Year's Day was just around the corner, she asked her yet again to take her with her, at least for the holiday season, but Mrs. Bird stubbornly refused.

"My friend living next door will call you if something bad happens to me," Mrs. Bird added. "She spends some time with me…"

"Mother decided to die," Anna thought and broke out in a cold sweat. "I'll be the one to blame if this happens. Everything started the moment I revealed my big secret. I don't know who's to blame, Mrs. Bird for changing my life along with my identity, or Sarah, who revealed my true identity to me as well as changed my whole existence?"

Anna's bad hunch was borne out on New Year's Day of 1967. Frieda was the first one to wake up to the phone ringing. At the other end of the line was Mrs. Bird's neighbour. Within a few minutes, Anna went through another sad patch in her life. Her favourite mother, the woman who raised and loved her like her own child, the woman who concealed her true name so that she would experience motherhood, was no longer with them. She had passed away in her sleep.

Anna awakened Adolf, told him what had happened, and they both left for her paternal home. Although there Adolf attended to all the funeral details, Anna stayed in her room for a while. She wanted to cry her eyes out alone without knowing why. She had mixed feelings right now…Still, she had to get all this over by herself.

Yet another chapter in Anna's life had come to a close with her mother's death. She realised that three days later, seated all alone in her favourite library…That's where she always snuggled to plunge into her thoughts. She still didn't know how she felt about that loss. She was in a lot of pain, no doubt, but how much more painful was the loss of her real parents? She wanted to believe that Mrs. Bird's death put an end to all that story, which was full of lies and hypocrisy. From now on, she would be able to carry on with her life by the side of the man who loved her more than anything else in the world and their beloved daughter. Still, she was hesitant. That indeterminate fear was a permanent burden on her chest.

"I still have Sarah," she faltered. "She was the one who told me that the truth, no matter how hard, is more valuable than a lie. I guess she's right."

The winter of 1967 was milder than the previous one. Helga was growing fast and had become an indispensable part of Anna's everyday life. She believed that all the difficulties she had been through were a thing of the past. Adolf spent more and more time with her. Sarah's health condition was stable now. The two women didn't see each other very often. Anna needed some time to herself. Besides, she didn't want to press the weak lady to tell her more. For the time being, she wanted to put the whole story on the back burner, although deep down, she couldn't forget about it. She would wait until Sarah herself talked to her.

What with her mother's death and the rest of her unfinished business, Emma, her best friend, had completely slipped her mind. She hadn't been able to talk to her at her mother's funeral, and now she felt the need to touch base. She had thought of talking to her about what she had been through, but the fact that Sarah didn't want her to talk to Adolf made her hesitant. What if she talked to Emma? If she revealed Sarah's secret as well, what would happen? Still, they could talk about Emma's job and personal life. Maybe it was better this way; it would take her mind off things. She called Emma on the spot and arranged to meet at their favourite place in the square in the afternoon.

"Welcome, Mrs. Krause!" exclaimed Emma when she saw her.

"Come on! Why are you doing this?" asked Anna laughingly.

"Let me take a look at you! You're stunning! I'm not going to complain about being neglected all this time, as I know you're going through a rough patch. I'm so sorry about your mother's loss. I don't know anything about her health condition, but I think she had an early death! I met her in my first year at the uni and felt like she was next of kin. Her loss must have cost you a lot!"

"Yes, my dear Emma, it did cost me a lot! Over the past months, I'd been aware of my mother's serious health issues and kept asking her to come over to my place. Still, she wouldn't hear about it. Her heart failed her. She couldn't take it. Now everything's over. I'm trying to close this circle and carry on with my family life. How are you doing? As Adolf is serious and discreet — you must have realised that already! —, he doesn't speak much about his work. Anything staggering in your life? Believe me; love's a most desirable earthquake!"

"I'm doing fine job-wise. As you said, Adolf offers me help as discreetly as he can. Love-wise, yes, something's going on, but I'm not sure yet. He's from the uni. When I make sure, I'll let you know. After all, you were and still are a real friend. I also want to remind you that I'll be there if you're having any trouble. I know you better than anyone else, right?"

"Thanks once again, sweetie. The truth is, there have been some issues lately, especially before and after Mrs. Bird's death, but it's all solved now and is a thing of the past. When the dust settles, we may talk about a little fairytale like the ones we used to read when we were little girls."

"Should I be worried?"

"No, no, I'm fine! Let's change the subject…One day, I want you to drop by and see Helga. She's grown up! You won't recognise her!"

CHAPTER EIGHTEEN

For Anna, that winter ran considerably smoothly with no further troubles. For the time being, she avoided visiting Sarah, but she called her frequently. She didn't say much about her life's tragic story as she believed there were no more discoveries to be made. She didn't have to rush to dig more into it. She also hoped her wounded heart would heal one day forever. Something inside told her that Sarah would be the one to get to the bottom of all this, sparing her all those nightmares. Anna would banish all her grim thoughts if she managed to learn something about her real parents' course of life — those people who were cut off in their prime so unabashedly and mercilessly. Then, when everything was over, Adolf, the only person who adored her, would help her get back to normal life so that the three of them would live together to the full.

Yet, life had another sad moment in store for her. This time, she had a phone call from the hospital, not a neighbour, as in her mother's case. A kind voice was heard at the other end of the line:

"Good morning. Could I speak to Mrs. Anna Krause?"

"Speaking."

"Mrs. Krause, I'm calling to let you know that Mrs. Andrea Emberhard has been rushed into hospital. She has severe respiratory insufficiency and she asked us to call you."

"Thank you very much. How serious is all this? I'll come over as soon as I can."

"Alright, Mrs. Krause. I inform you that she's in an extremely serious condition. That's all I can divulge. The doctors will tell you more."

Anna wanted to hang up straight away as Adolf was still there. Suddenly, though, she felt a lump in her throat upon hearing the woman's words. After a while, Adolf came downstairs for breakfast.

"Morning, love. Who called you at this time? You look upset!"

"Ah, nothing special, honey," she said and bent over to kiss him while trying to hide her agitation. "Well…you shouldn't be bothered about such matters. It's women's stuff. It was Emma."

"So early in the morning? Did anything happen to her?"

"No, don't think the worst. Well, something good has come up in her life, and…well, as I said, this is women's stuff. Don't tell her anything when you see her at school, OK? She doesn't want anyone to know yet."

"Alright, alright! You don't have to give me all the details. I just asked a simple question. I got it."

After a while, Adolf left and Anna hurriedly got dressed, informed Frieda that she would be away for a while, then dashed to the hospital. On her way there, she prayed to God that her friend could get well soon. If her condition was serious, as she was told, she hoped at least she would talk to her before she passed away.

In a while, she found Sarah in ward 203, together with another two gravely ill patients.

"You're late, sweetheart," Sarah told her in a barely audible voice.

"My sweet Sarah, I ran to you as soon as Adolf left for work. What happened to you? What do the doctors say?"

"Listen to me, my daughter. Come closer as I can barely talk. Listen to me and don't interrupt me. It's very hard for me to talk. Over the past few days, I've felt I'm at death's door. My lungs are torn apart and my heart won't take it for much longer. I don't need to hear that from the doctors. The flu I came down with a few days ago simply worsened my condition."

"Please open the drawer next to me and get an envelope with your name written on it. Well, my sweet daughter, these few days, I've been having second thoughts about messing up with your life. I was about to burn this envelope, along with the rest I keep at home. I finally burnt the others and, without knowing why I kept only this with all the details that concern you as well. Maybe I kept it because I believed I had to see all this through to the end, no matter what happened afterwards. I didn't want to take this big truth to my grave, no matter how harsh."

Anna spontaneously made to tear off the envelope, but Sarah held her hand to stop her.

"No, don't do it now. I have to speak to you first. You have to listen to me carefully. First of all, for one last time, I need to ask you if you still want to know about your parents and what exactly happened."

Agitated, Anna nodded her head, so Sarah continued:

"If you remember, I once told you that, after all those tragic things I've been through, I personally believe that harsh truth is preferable to a sweet lie. I don't know how much longer I will live. All these documents inside the envelope, I've kept them at home all these years. It's the evidence I've been gathering ever since I worked at the Ministry. At first, I didn't want to give it to you as the contents would harm your soul. You've been through a lot. Of course, I've already promised you, and even now, I don't know if I'm doing the right thing. Regardless of all these ups and downs that I've been having, though, two days ago I decided I would tell you about this envelope. Not now."

"What d'you mean?"

"As I'm beginning to get tired, I want to ask you one last time if you're ready to find out about some things that will answer your questions, but may harm your sensitive soul. So are you ready?"

Without a hint of terror or panic on her face, Anna nodded.

"Alright, then. Come closer, sweetie. I also want you to promise you'll open this envelope only after I'm gone. Do you promise?"

"Yes, but why not now? Are its contents so bad? I only want to know for a single reason: to heal my wounds and make sure my parents' souls find closure. After all this, I've promised myself to carry on with my life with my husband and daughter, leaving it all behind."

Sarah felt discomfort and chest pain at that very moment, so Anna ran to call the nurse. In a few minutes, the doctor stormed in while Anna, standing outside, could barely hear his voice, as he commanded that Sarah be rushed to the intensive care unit. Her stomach was in knots, just as tight as her fist that held the envelope. After two hours of anguish outside the ICU, Anna heard the bad news.

She stayed there all alone for quite some time. She wanted to cry, just like she did when her mother passed away. She would shed tears for the third time, just like she did back then when she was two months old in another country, her home country.

A few hours later, after she asked the hospital reception to call her if they needed anything, she left for home, carrying the heavy envelope that might hold the truths of her life. She didn't open it, though, out of respect for Sarah's last wish.

"I'll open it tomorrow morning when I'm alone. When Adolf and Frieda with Helga leave." She wanted to be all alone when she read those documents.

That night, she looked quite calm to Adolf. She feared that her agony might show on her face or in her movements. Seeing how calm she was, Adolf felt calm as well. By the same token, when he saw Anna angry or sad, especially after Mrs. Bird's death, he couldn't, but be overwhelmed with stress that made him overprotective, more than he used to be in the past. For Anna, this night seemed like an eternity. Although she was tired after her hard day in the hospital, she stayed up all night, staring at the ceiling till dawn.

In the morning, Adolf found her in the kitchen. As usual, she was waiting for him to have breakfast. After she had a cold bath to take strength, Anna didn't let her agitation show. Still, Adolf could see through her and asked her once again to calm down. If she needed anything at all, she could call him and he would be right there, but Anna was in a world of her own. After waiting for another couple of hours for Helga to wake up so that Freida could take her to the park, she wasted no time: she dashed to the library and took the envelope off the shelf where she had hidden it the previous day.

There were dozens of documents and yellowed sheets of paper inside. Apart from these, there was also a recently typed page — a letter from Sarah addressed to her.

"My dear Anna, this envelope contains very important documents I took from the Ministry where I was working before, during, and after the war. Besides, there are documents and reports of people that I collected through other compatriots. When you read these contents, you'll probably hate me but, when I saw you determined to find out the truth, I too made the big decision not to hide anything from you. I want you to know that the truth, no matter how harsh, must be spoken. The first time I met you and found out who you were, I swore to reveal the whole hypocrisy you were living. After a while, though, I regretted it and stepped back. Then, I thought of my own fake life and finally told you one of the truths you needed to know. You're so young and I thought you couldn't live with a false identity for the rest of your life as I did.

"Now, after all this pressure you went through, it's time to find out another one, a harsher one. If you're ready to accept what follows, keep reading. If not, burn this envelope right away and carry on with your life with your beloved husband and only daughter."

I knew from the start who you were, thanks to your father, Hans Meisner, as well as what became of your real parents, when they were executed, and how. Then, I started digging into the Ministry's archives and found the name of the one in charge of the executions. It wasn't only your parents who were killed, but hundreds of other Jews in Auschwitz. Your parents died piled up inside the gas chambers in Auschwitz, Poland, in 1943.

"I could stop here. Still, as I promised you, I would reveal every single detail; I'll tell you who the one in charge was. A high-ranking German official issued these orders to get the Jews executed. However, the one who ordered the executions on that tragic day was a young lowly S-S officer serving as head of the guard in that purgatory called Auschwitz. You'll find his name in an official document referring to the specific year: 1943. Let me repeat once again: if you don't want to move on, burn the envelope and stop here. Although I barely know you, I love you so much like my own child like the child God didn't bless me with."

Anna suddenly broke out in a cold sweat, a burden weighing down on her chest. Panicky, she started leafing through the documents. Within a few minutes, in a barely audible voice, she spelled the name of the one in charge of the crimes that were committed in that purgatory. The head of the gas chambers was Adolf Krause…

Still and white as a sheet, Anna dropped unconscious to the floor. As soon as she opened her eyes, her head reeling, she couldn't remember anything. A splitting headache forced her to slump to the couch.

"God, what happened?" she wondered. "Something bad must have happened to me. Maybe I dozed off and had a nightmare?!"

Looking around, she saw the documents scattered across the floor; it was then that she came back to reality. Searching, she found that document again and read it one more time, in case all this was just a bad dream. No, everything was the same, so was the name. She read it over and over again, hoping she had made a mistake.

Adolf, my God! Adolf! He was the executioner! The man she married and loved. Her daughter's father. The man she loved more than anyone else in the world. The man she swore to live with forever—the one who loved her so much and proved it every single minute and day.

"What do I do now? Fate had another tragedy in store for me! The worst of all. Now I have no one to help me. I'm all alone like back then when I came into this world. Back then, I cried out of fear. Now I can't even cry. I don't want to cry anymore."

She stood up with difficulty and went to the kitchen to make coffee, hoping it would give her a boost. She was still clutching that document in her sweaty palm. It was the piece of paper Sarah had left her to mark the end of both women's lives.

Anna came to realise what a dangerous turn her life had taken. Her previous traumas had made her less sensitive and harder.

"I have to get over this shock as Frieda will be back with Helga, and he will be here by noon. I have to come round and see what I can do. Right now, I feel too tired to think straight. I have to face the worst now!"

Even for a short while and under the pressure of time, these thoughts helped her get over the shock. All these traumas and reversals she had been through turned her heart to stone, which now made it easier for her to check her feelings. So when the others came back home, Anna was ready to deal with the situation, although she was crying inside her. She feigned discomfort and went up to her room as she didn't want Adolf to see her face, at least not at that particular moment.

As always, Adolf was worried and, when after almost two hours Anna came downstairs, he held her by the hand, sat on the couch in the living room, and told her:

"Sweetheart, I want you to know how much I love you and, whatever happens, because I'm sure something serious is going on now, I'll always be there for you. That beautiful student seated in the second row that I fell in love with, I will always love and protect until I die."

Upon hearing that man — her daughter's father, the one she adored — express his feelings in the most tragic moment of her life, she thought she was losing her mind. She felt she couldn't even open her mouth to speak. If she could, what words would she utter? She only cracked a bitter smile and lay back on the couch.

Unable to hide his puzzlement and preoccupation, Adolf stood up and went to Helga's room. After a while, Anna followed him and, after apologising, saying that she hadn't slept very well the previous night, she went to her room to lie down. She drifted off to sleep a few minutes later.

The following morning, Anna woke up at the same moment as Adolf, well-rested and determined to hide the new tragedy as well as she could. Above all, she owed that to Helga. She apologised to Adolf again, telling a white lie that she suddenly realised her mother's loss and that was the reason she acted like that. Of course, Adolf didn't seem to believe her. Anna asked him to leave her alone for a few days to get some rest as she felt exhausted. Then, she promised everything would run smoothly.

"You don't want to tell me what's going on, eh?" he asked her once again and, as he got no answer, he kissed her on the forehead this time and, just as he opened the door, he told her that he would respect her wish.

Anna needed some time to think. It was also Helga. That was the one she should think of right now. She felt the need to dive deep into her soul and pick up its leftovers, in case she managed to find her way out of that maze. In there, she would have to make her decisions. All alone, without her loved one since she felt the only person left in her life had already drifted apart.

After having Helga and Frieda go for a walk again, she went up to her room. Still, as she looked at the bed, she was overwhelmed with fear, so she ran down the stairs and lay on the couch in the library. She pulled the 'bleeding envelope' out of its hideout and, the moment she opened it, she decided to close it again.

"No, no, I shouldn't. I don't want to open it. I don't want to see what's inside of it. I have to make up my mind about what I'm going to do from now on. Once again, my life is hanging in the balance. My fate had it that I should live with a man who murdered my parents most brutally because of him, I'll never see them again. Yes, but he was merely a soldier carrying out orders. He had to obey; otherwise, they would kill him too. That was preferable to murdering thousands of people without a qualm. My father and mother must have suffered so much in those gas chambers till they died…"

A shiver went up and down her body. She rose from her seat and nervously paced up and down the room.

"Adolf's a murderer, a ruthless murderer," she whispered desperately. "As his behaviour has shown so far, he hasn't regretted all these crimes. Of course, he's hiding, probably because he doesn't know the truth about me. He can't know about my real origins that I come from a country he loves so much, according to the plays he teaches. Obviously, he doesn't know that among those innumerable people he murdered with his own hands were also his parents. For the time being, I shouldn't let it show. Not until I decide what to do. Whatever I have to do, I must do it really quickly."

She sat back on her chair, this time her hand grasping her favourite book, *Medea*.

"Why has fate made me adore this play?" she wondered. "This woman, the heroine, was a hurt woman who committed this heinous crime out of revenge, going through various stages until she committed a murder. As Adolf told us in his capacity as professor, she didn't do that for no reason. Is there anything that could justify a crime?"

Her soul was overwhelmed with so many confusing predicaments.

"I have to make up my mind quickly," she said to herself. "How can I live with a man who perpetrated so many crimes and killed so many innocent lives? God, what am I going to do? I have to choose between the man I loved with all my heart and a killer. Between my child's father and someone who's committed so many crimes. Between the truth and a lie. My mother, Mrs. Bird, and my husband concealed the truth. Sarah revealed everything to me, leading my life to an impasse. Still, after all these discoveries, my soul's dark. How can I carry on with my life like that?"

With time, Mrs. Bird's death brought balance to Anna's soul, as if a huge weight were lifted. What would she do now, though? How would she get rid of that new nightmare?

How would she be able to cleanse her soul of all that filth the new revelation brought? If she were to speak to Adolf, how would he react? How does a serial killer who carries on living as if nothing has ever happened to react when his crimes are revealed?

She shot to her feet and pulled the envelope off the shelf. Calmer, this time, started leafing through the documents. Reading the name 'Adolf Krause' did not affect her. She spelled it again and again, in case she made a mistake. Maybe Sarah did.

No, it was there, solid and real, his father's name turning up in many parts of the text. This man was present in many executions of that period.

"Adolf, the man I swore to live with to the bitter end, is the one who so unabashedly ordered to have hundreds of innocent people sent to prison and killed in gas chambers. Is there a human mind that can think of such a plan of wiping out life?"

The moment this thought flashed through her mind, Anna leapt from her seat, her face inscrutable, her eyes dry. She didn't want to cry; she wouldn't be able to, even if she wanted. Who would she cry over?

"No, I shouldn't carry this deep within for the rest of my life. I have to shake off this dirt. Only this way will I be able to move on and help Helga."

She got hold of the book again.

"What did that heroine do to put her mind at ease after her husband's affront? She took revenge. She thought this was the right thing to do, and she did it. Revenge…Adolf…Helga…"

The key in the lock and Helga's voices snapped her out of her thoughts, bringing her back to reality, a reality that was so different for her.

She hid the envelope on the shelf again and stepped out of the office. She felt like she was a different person now, which showed on her face. She was determined to do something that she still didn't understand or realise. She hugged and kissed Helga, telling Frieda to prepare her lunch. She would go out for a walk. If Adolf came back in the meantime, he should eat on his own, not wait for her. She wanted to walk, hoping that the cold wind would help her think straight. Maybe she would shake off that nightmare that had laid siege to her mind, eating away at it. She didn't want to discuss with anyone; she wanted to do it independently, whatever she was to do. She wanted to take full responsibility for her actions.

Her heart had already turned to stone. She didn't want to forgive anyone. They had taken her life away after some hardened criminals had killed her parents in cold blood. Before she even came into this world, her emotions had frozen her soul. Maybe it was the other way round; who knows? She may have come to realise the truths of this world much too soon.

Was everything so tangled up inside of her, or was it too crystal clear for her to stare at reality?

Revenge…Adolf…Helga…Mrs. Bird…Sarah…Her parents…What was she meant to keep?

"I have to make up my mind now," she whispered to herself as she walked around the park. She didn't care about anything else at the moment.

"Mrs. Bird, my second mother, died under the weight of her responsibilities. Sarah passed away with her conscience clear as she didn't conceal the truth — a truth that had turned her own life upside down. Still, it is the truth. My parents, my real parents, died, simply because some other people so decided. Adolf, even if he carried out orders, is still one of the worst war criminals. Helga, a piece of him, is my whole life. Revenge…An act of punishment…For him who killed like that for no reason. Not just a single man, but thousands. I have to make up my mind fast. I won't stand this sick situation for much longer…"

When she returned home late, Anna was a different person. For the first time, Adolf looked a little angry and snapped at her:

"Love, I've been observing you for months now, and I see your behaviour's getting worse by the day. I also see how indifferent you are. I thought I'd leave you alone for quite some time, in case you managed to find solutions to your problems, but I can't stand seeing you like this. I want and demand that you tell me what's going on with you. Whatever it is, we will sort it out together. You can't keep me in the dark since you know how much I love you. You always consulted me whenever you were preoccupied with something. Now you're keeping yourself to yourself. Why? This harms Helga too!"

Determined and with a cool head, Anna answered that, whatever it was, she would solve it on her own; he shouldn't worry.

"Thanks to you, I've learnt to make quick decisions about my life," she told him with a bitter smile and went up to her room, leaving Adolf with an expression of puzzlement and preoccupation.

She had made up her mind…

CHAPTER NINETEEN

The following days were considerably calm and uneventful. That was thanks to Anna's attempt to show that the problem was addressed. Still, this didn't seem to reassure Adolf, who looked wearied and preoccupied. He didn't stop lavishing love on her.

That morning of April 6th, Adolf woke up with a splitting headache and high temperature. Anna seemed to worry a lot, so she dashed to the nearest pharmacy to get him some medicine. She told him to call the doctor, but he refused, saying that it wasn't serious; as soon as he took his medicine, he would be alright.

The previous day, Frieda had asked for their permission to visit her parents, so Anna, after she made some hot tea, suggested that he stay in bed and get back to sleep. Adolf thanked her and tried to sleep again as he felt rather weak. Anna spontaneously bent over to kiss him, still having feelings for him.

"We're going to let you rest. As soon as Helga wakes up, I'll take her for a walk. We won't too long."

"Alright. It'll be better for me. I'll be quiet. Don't worry. By the time you get back, I'll feel much better."

After a while, Anna woke Helga up, fixed her breakfast, and told her they would play outside, which really made her daughter leap for joy.

When mother and daughter were ready at the door, Anna kissed Helga, asked her to wait there for a while, got back in, headed for the kitchen, and without hesitation, turned on the gas tap. Without even looking back, she grabbed hold of her daughter's hand and ran down the stairs, thus putting an end to her personal tragedy and turning over the page in her book of life.

Three hours later, calm and fearless, she returned home, believing that this horrible act had come to an end. When she opened the door, the pungent smell wafting in the air forced her to pull Helga back. After she masked her nose with a piece of cloth she had put at the entrance, she dashed into the kitchen to turn off the tap. Much to her surprise, she found Adolf's dead body lying there. After she turned off the tap, she ran outside, grabbed Helga's hand, and asked for her neighbours' help, saying that something bad had happened. She pleaded with Mrs. Edda to keep her daughter for a while and went back.

Icy-cold and calm, she opened the windows and doors and called the Police and an ambulance. Within a few minutes, the police arrived, only to confirm Adolf's death. A while later, the doctor who arrived at the scene confirmed that the cause of death was a gas leak.

Anna reported exactly what happened to the Police, saying that he was off colour and stayed behind to sleep. Obviously, he went downstairs to have something hot to drink and, as the stove was on the blink, he used the gas, which eventually killed him. She justified her calmness, saying that she didn't want her daughter to realise that something bad had happened. She had made sure there was damage to the kitchen as well as a teapot on the stove.

In a while, after the ambulance left for the morgue, Anna said goodbye to the police officer, saying she would be at his disposal, and waited inside the house until that obnoxious smell went away before she brought Helga. She still hadn't fully realised that today she had written her name on the list of hardened criminals...

She couldn't stop thinking of Helga. What would she tell her? How would she talk to her? How would she react? She hadn't thought of all this before she made the decision to commit this crime. She still hadn't realised that her actions didn't differ from what Adolf had done to her parents. Yet, she couldn't and didn't want to think of all this right now. Her heart had turned to stone, shaking off all her feelings for him, and that's what had led her to this decision. She didn't fear that she would make a mistake...

As time heals all, two months after that new tragedy, Anna, lavishing love on her daughter, managed to bring some equilibrium to Helga's sensitive soul.

Anna herself had no remorse. She didn't even sense Adolf's absence; he was the man who had made her so happy and miserable. She hadn't made up her mind whether she would stay in that house. Everything was left exactly as it was on that day.

The summer was drawing closer. Still, it was a different summer. Two years before, she had lived a dream with him while the previous one was a nightmare. During this summer, she was living alone in a house, just like back then when, two months old, she was crying in another house. Then, someone had saved her life. Now she had to strive by herself from scratch. She would fight for her own life, but mainly for Helga, Adolf's daughter.

Of all her friends, only Emma, her best friend, had stayed behind. She couldn't believe that such a calamity had befallen Anna and the academic community. Anna didn't reveal any of those tragic moments to Emma, nor would she ever do that. She decided on that when she put her plan into action.

This summer, under pressure from her tragedy, she accepted Emma's suggestion that the three of them spend their summer holiday in a beautiful Spanish resort. She wanted to get away from home as she had begun to suffocate in there. When she came back, she would see what she could do about it.

Despite her efforts to create a pleasant atmosphere, though, Emma drew a blank. Therefore, she spent more time with Helga, letting Anna be. Her friend's loneliness had left its marks on her.

Things were much harder when they got back home, although Emma did all she could to show her that she would always be by her side. Now her new life began to dawn on Anna. It would be a life full of pain and hurdles. For the rest of her life, she would have to carry the burden of her guilt. Her act was actuated by revenge. She had murdered her loved one, the father of her daughter, the man she had deprived Helga of forever.

"How different is my act from his?" Anna wondered that morning, seated as she was in her favourite library, words barely coming out of her icy soul. "How will I carry on with my life without him? I pinned my dreams and hopes on him. How will I look at Helga's face every day, keeping under wraps this horrible truth for the rest of my life? How different will I be from Mrs. Bird, who actually concealed the truth for the sake of saving a life? Is it enough justification that I committed this heinous crime in order to punish someone for their worse crimes? Aren't all crimes the same when they take people's lives? Have I cleansed my soul through this act? Didn't I become an accomplice of all those people who sullied my soul? Shouldn't I feel guilty now? Did I have the right to take the life of a man, even if he was a hardened criminal of innocent souls? That's what Medea did. She did it out of revenge. So did Orestes. He killed his mother to avenge his father's murder. He cited that as an example when I asked him what remorse is. I was referring to my mother, Mrs. Bird, back then. He then told me that in this work, the writer wanted to show that when someone commits a crime, then they are forever haunted by remorse and cannot find closure."

As all these thoughts came rushing in, she broke out in a cold sweat and leapt to her feet, hoping to get rid of her regrets. In doing so, she dropped to the floor a book left on the desk from that tragic day. She hadn't been inside that room ever since. As she bent over to pick it up, she stumbled upon 'Medea' again, and in her attempt to open it, she came across a small white envelope on the first page. Puzzled as she was, she opened it. There was a letter inside addressed to her. With trembling hands, she began to read:

"My beloved Anna,

When I saw a beautiful young girl years ago inside that amphitheater, I fell in love with her and wanted to make her mine, the woman of my life. When I realised the feeling was mutual, I felt happy for the first time. When she gave me an equally beautiful daughter, then I was over the moon.

Still, human fate has different designs. What I mean is, now that you are alone and what has stigmatised your life is crystal clear, I want to tell you the whole truth and help you from up there to carry on with your life together with our beloved daughter, without regrets or guilt. I knew what you were going through from the start. Your mother, Mrs. Bird, told me a few days before she died. I found out who you were and what your real parents were, then my mind scurried back to some creepy moments of my life. I searched and found out. I didn't know what to do. I felt so weak for the first time. You could have forgiven Mrs. Bird for what she did. She saved your life and changed your name. While your mother changed your fate, though, another person, loyal to the ideas of a criminal system, was sent to death hundreds of thousands of innocent lives, among them your real parents.

I didn't seek to find who informed you about all this, but it didn't matter as it was all true. I often tried to convince myself to speak to you. I would tell you about my own remorse and how cowardly it was of me not to be able to assume my responsibilities and go to court. Still, I couldn't account for my actions to you, even if I was only eighteen back then, and the war was raging. This fate that led me to order the execution of all those innocent people that day is the same fate that brought your parents to those gas chambers.

Therefore, I went into academia, hoping that I would heal my wounds and save myself this way. When I met you, I believed you would be the one who would heal my wounds. As you see, though, a fate almost always writes its own story for each one of us. As I write these lines, I'm seated in the office, your favourite room. The house is filled with the gas you opened on your way out. I realised you were determined, just like your heroine, who's right next to me. The pungent smell woke me up; I came downstairs and realised what you had done. I can save myself right now, but a few minutes ago, I made a big decision.

I broke the stove, to make it look more convincing that it was me who used the gas, took one of the sleeping pills I've been using lately, and in a while, I will go to sleep on the floor, next to the stove, closing all the doors and windows and opening the gas tap.

I don't want you to feel any guilt in the future. You're not a murderer. As you tried to cleanse yourself, you showed me the way, even now. I want you to live with our angel for many many years, and always be truthful to her. Once, in a city restaurant, listening to a great musician's work, we both swore to live together to the bitter end. Still, as is always the case in the plays I used to teach and real life, fate often rules the end.

I want you to love Helga the way you loved me. This love may lift all the weights off your shoulder with time. You were burdened with so many problems at an early age..."

For one last time, Anna slumped onto the couch, her eyes misty. She couldn't believe what she had just read. She looked at the piece of paper again lying at her feet and read it one more time to check if all this was a new nightmare.

"It's his handwriting," she whispered. That tragic moment of his life, his remorse, and his love for her led her to assume all responsibility for his own death. "He did it to save me and help me live. Once again, someone tried to save me."

She burst into tears after all this time that she had been trying to keep them in check. This outburst made her heart lighter as she lifted all that weight off her chest, even for a short while.

After standing still on the couch for a while, she rose, got hold of Sarah's envelope, and the letter of the only person she loved and always would. She made for the fireplace where she set fire to them, consigning to oblivion her own tragedy, which was in three acts, just like another one written in her country thousands of years back…

CHAPTER TWENTY

"Mum, it's over. Let's get out of here."

As if snapping out of a nightmare, Anna leapt to her feet in fright.

"Ten years have passed already?" she stammered.

"What did you say, mum?"

"Nothing, sweetheart…Let's go…"

Worming her way through the crowd, she went down the narrow stone-built alley, but for an instant, she was gripped by thoughts once again.

"Where am I going now?" she wondered. "Back then that autumn, when I stepped into the amphitheatre for the first time, I thought I'd live a life full of dreams. Everything was so beautiful back then…A good friend, the first and only love of my life, a wedding, our daughter's birth, my mother, Mrs. Bird that I still love, my parents I never knew, the reversals I went through, the hard decisions, the purification of the soul, the guilt he wanted to shake off, although in the plays he taught he said no one ever gets away…"

"I miss him. He could have been saved, but he preferred to save my soul rather than his own. At the uni, he often talked to us about catharsis, the purification of the soul, and how this can be achieved. He followed his fate because he was afraid of carrying his own guilt and tried to spare me mine."

The awe-inspiring scenery suddenly frightened her.

"I was left alone. If I hadn't found out about all this, maybe that sense of bliss I felt would have been real amid all these lies."

Her legs grew heavy.

"What will come next? Where am I going now? How will I stand all these memories? What about the remorse? No, just before he died, he told me to carry on, but can you get away with guilt?"

"Mum, you're hurting me."

Anna snapped out of her thoughts. Her hand was clutching her daughter's hand. As she boarded the bus, the voices of the people around her brought her back to reality. One last look at the majestic sacred theatre, where she had seen the third and last act of an ancient tragedy moments earlier. Maybe it was her own tragedy.

Smothering her pain deep inside, she sat in the back and hugged Helga.

"Now we're going back home, sweetheart. We're going to the place where you were born, where I hugged you for the first time like I'm hugging you now. That's where dad enjoyed your presence, and we're going to live for the rest of our lives. And I promise your life will be much better than mine and your dad's."

The sun was high in the sky, drenching that beautiful place, Anna's home country. One last glance out the plane window. Maybe she would never come back here if she wanted to forget.

The following morning, although she was tired from the flight, she woke up early. She checked on Helga, who was fast asleep and went down to the kitchen to make some hot coffee. She then sat in the living room. Frieda was coming the next day. Maybe she would give her more days of leave for the summer. She wanted to be left alone for some time to take care of Helga around the clock. She felt the need to do so.

What about him who gave meaning to her life, who came like a real dream? Where was he now? The house was so empty without him...

"God, how am I going to live now, after all this, after what I've done? If all this hadn't happened...I think the truth is much worse than a lie, after all. I was happy before all this. Before I met Andrea, why did she have to tell me about the lie I lived in? Maybe to take revenge for her own tragedy and maybe because she wanted to break free from her own lie. Perhaps, through me, she wanted to put an end to the tragedy of an entire world."

But was this the end or the beginning of another tragedy for Anna?

Back then, at the age of two months, all alone in a house so far away from there, fate played a nasty trick on her...

Now she was alone in a house, crying — who knows for how long...

The pain she felt was unbearable, and so was remorse. She had to find the strength to carry on, and the only reason was Adolf's daughter. She had to spend even more time with her now, in hopes that she might be able to make up for the wasted time. She had to make sure Helga's life didn't end up the same way.

All of a sudden, a shiver went up and down her spine, just like it did in the past.

"What if I make the same mistake my mother and Adolf did? Will I keep under wraps what happened to Helga's father? And, if I reveal the truth to her, where will this lead us? To a new tragedy? The real mother I never knew brought me to life, but Mrs. Bird saved me. Sarah revealed the truth, probably to take revenge on the fate of her own family. I didn't hold Mrs. Bird a grudge because she saved me from certain death; there was no way she could have asked me if I wanted to be rescued. I had true feelings for Adolf and we swore to stick together to the bitter end. Still, I didn't honour my pledges and, through his death, he wanted to deliver me from my guilt. My fate was sealed the moment I was born. Is this how people's fate is written? My life was a small circle and it seems to me that it was closed really fast."

Anna tried to strike a balance between the truth and the lies. She didn't want to tell her daughter what had happened exactly — at least now that Helga was so young. How would she ever pluck up the courage to speak to her?

"How can I keep this under wraps? I'm afraid I won't be able to stand it. If I don't, how different will I be from all the rest?"

She shot to her feet, took a few steps into the living room, and as always, she made up her mind within a few minutes.

"Yes, but I can write to her. I'll write about all this in a book, a novel, a long one. This book will speak of life, my short life, that is, all my truths, and all the lies of a heroine called Anna. It'll be like an ancient tragedy. This book will only have a single copy, and I'll hand it to a single person: Helga, the daughter of two tragic people that fate wanted to live so near…and yet so far…"

THE END

I would like to thank the visual artist and friend Dimitra Fotopoulou for kindly crafting the book cover, my sister Angeliki as she was the first one to read the manuscript, and urge me to get the book published, my special friends, who put up with my endless prattle while I was writing it up, and finally my beloved daughter Nectaria. Thanks to her persistence, this novel was completed in my limited free time when I got back from my demanding job.